THE CONTINUUM CHRONICLES:
OF DEATH AND DESTINY

To Denise & Mark
Best wishes
From Dave

David N. Mayo

22 April 2013

THE CONTINUUM CHRONICLES:
OF DEATH AND DESTINY

DAVID N. MAYES

Copyright © 2013 by David N. Mayes.

Library of Congress Control Number: 2013900148
ISBN: Hardcover   978-1-4797-7433-3
               Softcover   978-1-4797-7432-6
               Ebook   978-1-4797-7434-0

All rights reserved. No part of this book may be reproduced or transmitted in any form or by any means, electronic or mechanical, including photocopying, recording, or by any information storage and retrieval system, without permission in writing from the copyright owner.

This is a work of fiction. Names, characters, places and incidents either are the product of the author's imagination or are used fictitiously, and any resemblance to any actual persons, living or dead, events, or locales is entirely coincidental.

Rev. date: 03/12/2013

To order additional copies of this book, contact:
Xlibris Corporation
1-800-618-969
www.Xlibris.com.au
Orders@Xlibris.com.au
502929

CONTENTS

Chapter 1	The Plot Is Laid	9
Chapter 2	The Assassins' Journey	15
Chapter 3	Death of a Witch and the Killing of an Emperor	24
Chapter 4	A Journey through Hell and the Prince's Escape	35
Chapter 5	Heroic Last Stand and the Monitor's Refuge	47
Chapter 6	Taming of the Wild Creatures and the Village Encounter	62
Chapter 7	Primitive Times and Adventures on the Monitor's Planet	73
Chapter 8	Global Warming and Economic Woes	85
Chapter 9	Global Conflict and Escape to the Mountains	101
Chapter 10	Visit of the Watchers and Global Recovery	116
Chapter 11	Final Resistance and a Journey through Time and Space	128
Chapter 12	Destruction of the Dinosaurs and a New Beginning	138

ACKNOWLEDGMENT

To my wife, for her unwavering support and patience in the production of this book and encouragement to never give up and keep on going to the end. My three sons for making me proud of their accomplishments, which encouraged me to keep on going and achieve my dreams.

CHAPTER 1

The Plot Is Laid

The sun was shining brightly and streamed through the huge throne room windows, like a light from heaven and bathed the room in glorious summer sunshine. It put Emperor Kyranus in a relaxed and optimistic mood, especially with the drink poured into him by Baron Lysandros. Baron Lysandros was resplendent in a light blue tunic with magnificent gold decoration and a matching cloak, which had a white fur trim, and it set off to advantage his tall muscular frame. He wore beautifully handmade sandals, inlaid with gold piping. Despite the expert cut and fit of the emperor's purple and gold tunic, decorated with the royal crest and magnificent purple cloak, he looked incongruous and overblown. His excessively obese figure and purple face clearly showed his love of good food and drinks and generally excessive life style. Like the baron, the emperor wore a beautiful pair of handmade sandals with an exquisite gold decoration.

Confident his plans had been carefully laid, having left no margin for error, the cunning baron considered he was in complete control. Brimming with confidence, he casually opened the conversation.

"Why did you appoint Captain Paniakos to be in charge of the empress's personal bodyguard, Your Majesty? What will happen at your soirée on Pleasure Island, as a result? You know how intensely they dislike each other?"

The Emperor chuckled. "They'll be so busy watching each other it will take the attention of the empress off me. I'm sick of her constant complaining about my excessive eating, drinking, gambling, and other pleasurable pursuits. Don't you think it is a clever plan?"

"Brilliant," replied the baron. "I never thought Your Majesty capable of such cunning behavior. However will the empress allow the captain to accompany her at the soiree, on Pleasure Island?"

"Oh yes, I will make sure he is there," chuckled the emperor. "Anyway, there is so much to do on Pleasure Island. It should be easy to avoid the empress. There is the gambling, the beautiful women, the fabulous entertainment, the wonderful food, and of course, the huge quantities of wine and other beverages. Yes, I will have a great time there."

Sometime later, the baron conducted a secret meeting with his four hired assassins. It was conducted in the baron's private hunting lodge, deep in the forest, well away from prying eyes. In keeping with the baron's focus on grand pure white granite, mined from a nearby quarry, the interior consisted mainly of white marble with more than enough rooms to cater for his important guests. It was full of beautiful marble statues and magnificent frescoes. A key feature of the central courtyard was a magnificent water fountain, fed by an underground creek, running through the property. The courtyard was also resplendent with a range of exotic plants and olive and fruit trees.

It only took one look to identify the assassins; they were a wild lot, with scruffy beards and hair that looked totally unkempt. They each wore a dirty tunic, the colors of which were barely discernible under the layers of dirt. They also wore boots that were covered in grime and very much the worse for wear. They each exuded a disgusting smell, and the clean and wholesome slave—with spotless tunic and clean sandals—displayed his obvious disgust as he led the assassins into the presence of the baron. When refreshments had been served to his guests, the slave was dismissed with instructions that they were not to be disturbed. The baron then turned to the assassins.

"I require confirmation that you have successfully accomplished the assignment I set you before I provide the agreed payment in gold."

"Indeed, My Lord, apart from viewing the head of Baron Nilanova in the sack I am holding, would it please you to know all of the details?" inquired the chief assassin named Damos.

"Yes, of course it would. I look forward with great satisfaction to hearing how my archenemy, Baron Nilanova and his sons, who represent the biggest threat to my scheme to destroy the royal family, has been eliminated for good," responded the baron.

The chief assassin lifted the head of Baron Nilanova out of the sack, by the hair and held it aloft, for viewing by the baron. He then put the head back into the sack and began a detailed account of the assassination.

"We did as you instructed and kidnapped the girl, whom Baron Nilanova's youngest son is sweet on. I sent her handmaiden into the tavern, where the baron and his four sons were drinking. And she gave a note, as instructed to the youngest son. The note said that his sweetheart, Akalada, wanted to discuss something of importance. The youngest son knew that protocol would preclude her being able to enter the tavern and communicate directly with him. So the youngest son made his excuses to the rest of his family and came out of the tavern to meet the lady Akalada. He did not see us lurking in the shadows until too late, and by that time, I brought the cudgel down on his head and knocked him senseless. We brought him back to his senses and then proceeded to torture him, making sure we cut up his handsome face. We made sure he had the chance to escape, and he limped as fast as he could into the tavern. His face, in particular, was a terrible sight, and the blood was pouring out of him. On entry to the tavern, the sight of him caused the females present to scream in horror. The incensed baron called for his soldiers, who were supposedly drinking and playing dice in a back room, as was their custom. However, we had bribed one of the slaves to drug the guards' wine, and they were unconscious, sprawled across the table on which they had been gambling. The baron was in such a towering rage that he did not hesitate and raced out of the tavern, followed by his sons. Hernagos threw his lance and pinned the baron's oldest son to the tavern door. The lance had penetrated his heart, and we knew he would not be involved in any subsequent fight with us. The baron thus had only the two fully fit sons out of the four to fight with us. Despite this, they fought with great ferocity and proved to be able swordsmen. However, we finally dispatched them, and they lay dead in the street, outside the tavern. I cut off the baron's head and placed it in this sack before we left. So any threat they may have posed to you is now ended."

"You have done well, and I am extremely pleased," responded the baron. "However, that is only phase one. You now have to ensure that phase two is successfully accomplished, specifically to take care of the royal family and thus facilitate my seizure of the throne."

The four assassins were then handed their payment, in gold, and given comprehensive instructions by the baron. When it was completed, he said, "You have all been thoroughly briefed, so I can assume that you know exactly what to do?" To reinforce what he had been saying, the baron emphasized, "The royal galley must be totally destroyed while the royal entourage is sleeping in the nearby house. This is to provide the means to distract the emperor's guards, while you enter the house and assassinate the royal family. It is also vital that none of the emperor's guests who have been invited to his soiree have the means of travel to Pleasure Island."

"We will not let you down, and in turn, you will ensure the captain of your soldiers has the gold to reward us for our work? We want to be well away before the death of the royal family becomes generally known," said Damos.

"Don't worry," replied the baron. "Detailed preparations have been made, and my troops will be there to support you when you assassinate the royal family. I look after those people who serve me well. Now leave, and as instructed, you will make your way through the forest to the dock side to ensure you are not seen. Remember, at the insistence of the very determined Baron Nilanova's wife, the baron's soldiers will be undertaking an intensive search for you. You can also be sure that there will be witnesses from the tavern who will have given detailed descriptions of you all to the soldiers."

The baron glanced at the leader of the assassins, Damos, and asked, "However, before you go, you're certain Hernagos here can safely lead you through the forest?"

"My Lord, I have explored all aspects of the forest since I was a boy and know every route through it," interposed Hernagos.

"Very well then, you can all be on your way. And Damos, take this sack with you and ensure you properly dispose of the head in the forest."

The baron returned to his castle after the assassins had left the hunting lodge. He called for a goblet of wine and settled into his favorite chair in a relaxed mood. His wife noted his calm, relaxed outlook. "So, you have had a profitable day, husband?"

"I certainly have. It is now only a matter of time before the emperor and his family members are all dead, and I am the real power in Atlantis," he responded. His confidence grew with the thoughts of his cleverness and how his treachery was so obviously flawless in its planning. He called on his manservant to fill up his goblet with more wine and leisurely sipped it with a sly gloat on his face.

The morning of the royal gathering, the baron sent a messenger with a letter of apology to the emperor. He pointed out that the whole of his family was sick and the symptoms were similar to that of an early onset of the plague.

"I am impressed that the baron has been so quick to apologize for his proposed inability to attend the royal function due to his family's sickness. Hopefully it will not be the plague. However, just in case, we must take the necessary precautions and ensure we stop its spread, so make sure the baron's castle is properly quarantined. Kill anyone trying to leave the castle and stop anyone who is trying to enter," instructed a very concerned emperor to his chief adviser.

"It shall be as you order, Your Majesty," replied the chief advisor. "If you will excuse me, I will ensure that troops are dispatched straight away."

The emperor nodded his approval, and the chief advisor bowed low and hurried away. The chief advisor instructed the captain of the emperor's guard, and soon a troop of soldiers were on their way to take up position at the entrance of the castle. When the captain of the guard was satisfied that the castle was properly guarded, he left, after ensuring that the soldiers were informed of when they would be relieved.

Baron Lysandros called on his closest aide and ordered him to check out the soldiers at the castle gates and report back to him.

"There are some twenty soldiers dispersed around the exterior of the gate, my Lord. I believe if we leave by the secret exit, our soldiers can work their way around and either bypass or encompass them," responded the baron's aide.

"Good, then we will wait until the troops return that I have dispatched to the emperor's departure point for Pleasure Island, where the royal galley is moored. And if we have any problems, we will kill the soldiers guarding our gate," replied the baron.

CHAPTER 2

The Assassins' Journey

Subsequent to leaving Baron Lysandros's hunting lodge, the four assassins made their way through the forest. The huge trees provided a thick canopy and made the woods a dark and forbidding place, striking fear into the hearts of the assassins. To make matters worse, the constant rain over the last month had resulted in thick, almost impenetrable undergrowth so the journey was very slow going. The assassins' mood turned dark as they became increasingly frustrated. Despite this, they slowly but surely made progress through the forest.

Suddenly, disaster struck when the ground unexpectedly gave way under Hernagos. He screamed in fear as he fell into a deep pit, onto a bed of upraised, sharp, pointed stakes. The stakes dove through his body and blood spurted up from the wounds, and death quickly overcame the agonized assassin.

The chief assassin stood with hands on hips, glaring into the pit at the pierced body of his companion. "Hernagos has fallen into a trap set for a wild boar. A curse on the miserable peasants who built this pit. Just let me get at them, and they will regret that they had ever existed."

Suddenly Damos realized that he was still carrying the sack containing Baron Nilanova's head, fastened to his back pack which contained his food and water. He opened up the sack and threw it and its grisly contents into the pit. "Here, Hernagos, someone to keep you company."

The assassins howled with laughter at this remark; however, it seemed to be more to break the tension than enjoy the humor.

"What do we do now?" inquired the assassin named Leonardos of his leader.

"We push on, traveling toward the sun until we either meet someone who can direct us out of this accursed forest, or we meet a pathway to take us out," responded Damos.

"The light is fast fading, Damos. What do we do when it gets dark?' inquired a concerned Leonardos.

Before the chief assassin could respond, Armosthenes—one of the other assassins—excitedly cried out, "Look! A hut not too far in front of us. Let's hurry!"

They rushed ahead with renewed vigor and soon came to a clearing with a roughly built wooden hut in the center. It was in a really dilapidated condition and looked as though it was about to collapse. The wooden walls were twisted, with every length of timber grossly deformed and covered in green mold. Outside the entrance of the hut sat a very old woman, her face showing the marked effect of the ravages of time, stirring the contents of a cooking pot from which a delicious-smelling aroma arose. The hungry assassins rushed forward, and the old woman looked up at them with watery eyes.

"I knew you were on the way. I was warned of your coming when I read the cards," said the old woman.

"Did your cards also tell you we were hungry and would slit your throat unless you fed and sheltered us?" snarled the chief assassin.

"Oh yes, they warned me that you were ruthless and very evil men, but I could not escape. Apart from the fact that I move very slowly, I have nowhere else to go. However, I will feed you. There is more than enough rabbit stew, and the special vegetables in the stew will really whet your appetite," responded the woman. "You can sleep in the hut. I've laid down extra ferns from the forest floor, and I'll sleep in the far corner of the dwelling."

Once the assassins had eaten their fill and were feeling quite relaxed, a curious Damos inquired, "How did you come to live in the forest, old witch? I assume it was not from choice?"

"Once, I lived in Darium, the nearest village to here. I was the village healer and spiritual guide, and I had a close affinity with the gods, and they provided me with guidance in my work. I cured the sick and read the cards to help those in trouble. In return, the villagers made sure that I had a good supply of vegetables and fowls, and occasionally meat when a wild boar or deer was captured and killed. They dig pits in the forest, which ensure the provision of a regular supply of pork," said the witch.

"We know," said the chief assassin grimly. "That's how we lost our companion, when he fell into one of the villagers' pits—a really horrible way to die. Anyway, if you were doing so well, how did you end up here?"

* * *

One day, the plague struck quite unexpectedly and the villagers were dropping like flies. Unknown to us, it was virulent in the surrounding villages. So Diaphones, one of the villagers returning from a trading trip to a couple of the surrounding villages must have inadvertently brought it back with him. I tried all of my medicines and potions, but nothing worked. Then an elderly man, known as the Monitor, arrived at the village. He had a supply of what he called the fluid of life, and this worked a miraculous cure. When drunk by the infected person, his health immediately improved, and after further rest, he was completely cured. The Monitor advised that the hut in which the person subject to the plague was residing should be completely cleared and cleaned out and all clothing and bed sheets used by this person should be burned.

The Monitor left the village when it appeared that every person subject to the plague was cured. However, one of the villagers approached me and said his eldest son had suddenly gone down with the disease. Fortunately, I had a few bottles of the fluid of life given to me by the Monitor and was able to bring about a cure. The villager was truly grateful and made a promise to assist me if I was in trouble, no matter what it cost. Events transpired that caused him to take great risks in order to meet this commitment.

On the day of the village market, Euladius, the eldest son of the local land owner, came galloping into the village on his charger accompanied by six of his companions, as was his wont. I was in a makeshift tent as was my habit on market day. The villagers would visit me in the tent if they required medicine or basic healing. I would also read the cards for them if they were anxious about the future or required advice.

As I came out of the tent to have a breath of fresh air, Euladius came racing up and knocked me flat. Fortunately, I was not too badly injured as it was only a glancing blow from his steed. Euladius reined in his horse and towered over me and sent a torrent of abuse my way and directed a stream of phlegm into my face as I tried to rise. When I finally managed to get back on my feet, he lashed me across the face with his whip. He then said, "This will remind you not to get in the way of Euladius, you old witch. Next time you will not be so lucky and will taste the edge of my sword."

I cursed him for his arrogance and vicious behavior and told him that he would come to a bad end, which would involve his horse. He and his companions laughed in my face and rode off into the marketplace. In customary fashion, they left their horses at the village livery stable and made their way on foot into the market, going from stall to stall. They bullied and harassed each stall holder, with increasing derisory behavior, helping themselves to whatever they fancied off each stall. No one dared to challenge them, as the villagers feared the local land owner, who was a particularly vicious individual. Eventually, they tired of this game, and Eladius challenged his six companions to a horse race in a nearby paddock. He offered to pay anyone who beat him a bag of gold, so they lined up for the race with obvious enthusiasm. When they were lined up, the horses snorted, chomped on their bridles, and stomped their feet in eager anticipation of the demands to be made of them. The riders bent forward, ready for the off, determined that the bag of gold would be theirs at the race's conclusion. At the shout of go by the villager co-opted as the race starter, the riders urged their horses into a fast gallop. The riders yelled and screamed in excitement and lashed their mounts and each other as they jostled to secure the lead.

However, it was Euladius that finally broke away from the pack and raced into the lead with a loud cry of triumph, and the other riders spurred their steeds on in an effort to catch him. As he neared the winning post, Euladius, well ahead of the other riders, turned to mock them. With his attention divided, he did not see the almost-hidden pothole just ahead and suddenly found himself flying over the horse's head as its foot was trapped in the hole. There was a loud snap as the horse's leg almost broke in half with the forward momentum. Euladius could do nothing to lessen his forward movement and crashed head-first into a large boulder, fracturing his skull and breaking his neck. He lay still, and his companions, who had raced up to him and dismounted, discovered he was dead. Eusabius, one of the riders was panic-stricken.

"How do we tell Myrocalese that his son is dead? We were responsible for keeping him safe. He will have us all tortured and fed to the wild animals of the forest."

"Don't panic, Eusabius, there is only one person responsible for Euladius's death, and that is that ugly old witch in the village. If we concoct a suitable supporting story, we will be completely free from punishment, and the witch will get what is coming to her for putting a curse on Euladius. We'll also seize two of the villagers—the threat of torture and death to their families will provide the necessary incentive for them to support our story. So Eusabius and Miltonius, you will go to the Lord Myrocalese and inform him of his son's death and bring him here, but say as little as possible. We will provide full details when he arrives at the scene of his son's demise," exclaimed Metrodius, another of the riders.

By the time one of the riders had appraised the land owner of the details of his son's death and returned to the site of the accident with him, a suitable story was concocted by the remaining riders. The land owner rode up, accompanied by a detachment of his soldiers. The grief-stricken father took his son's body in his arms and openly wept for a long period of time. When he had finally recovered his composure, the land owner turned to the riders in a towering rage.

"You were supposed to take care of my son, and now he is dead. You will have plenty of time to regret this incident when you are subject to unbearable pain and suffering."

Metrodius swallowed hard before speaking. "Surely, My Lord, the actual person responsible for your son's death should be punished, not us, your loyal followers."

The land owner peered suspiciously at Metrodius, "What do you mean the real person responsible for my son's death?"

"My Lord," went on Metrodius, 'the wrinkled old witch cursed your son when he brushed past her, when riding through the village. She called up demons from hell, a terrible sight to behold. They were black as night, covered in slimy, oily scales, with the most terrible countenance and each stood on cloven hooves. The demons cackled and laughed horribly, while the witch placed a curse on your son saying that he would be thrown from his horse and killed. See I have brought two of the peasants from the village to verify our story."

The land owner glared at Metrodius and his five companions and the two peasants. "Is this true?" he roared.

The six riders and both villagers, who were visibly shaking and quaking with fear, nodded their silent agreement.

"Then go and bring this witch to me. I suppose you know where she is to be found?" the land owner asked in a voice that demanded a positive response.

"She will still be at the fair, My Lord, carrying out her evil work in a tent adjacent to the stalls," said Metrodius. "I will take two of my companions and bring her to you."

He then selected two of the other riders, and they mounted their steeds and raced off to the village.

I was in my tent, providing healing advice to a villager and his wife and, as part of this process, handing out herbal medicine when the land owner's three men burst into the tent.

"So, witch, you once again are practicing the black arts and giving evil potions to these innocent villagers?" screamed the one they called Metrodius. "Well, we will soon put an end to that!" He picked up my bag and peered into it, saying, "So this is where you keep your evil black magic aids?" And he swept the herbal cures, cards, and other items on the table into the bag.

Metrodius seized me by the scruff of the neck, and he grabbed a torch from a nearby market entertainer and set fire to my tent. The nearby stall holders grabbed up their wares in panic and moved them as far away from the flames as possible. Some of them grabbed buckets and filled them with water from a nearby well and attempted to control the fire.

Meanwhile, one of Metrodius's companions had mounted his steed, and Metrodius and the other man lifted me in front of the mounted rider. Oh how I struggled and cursed, but it was of no use; they were too powerful for me.

They rode back to the land owner and threw me onto the ground. Metrodius threw my bag onto the grass next to me, saying, "My Lord, there is the witch, the cause of your son's death. I have also brought her bag of black magic accompaniments. What shall we do to punish her for your son's murder?"

"Oh, I know exactly what to do about that, but first of all, what has happened to my son's horse?" inquired the land owner.

"It is over there, My Lord, but it will have to be destroyed, its leg is badly broken and will never heal, and it is in agony," responded the rider named Miltonius.

"Very well, go and put it out of its misery with your sword. A sad end to a fine animal. It was a birthday gift to my son from me. Once you have killed the steed, cut off its head. I intend to put it to good use, as part of the witch's punishment," ordered the land owner.

"Nikallernor, my torturer, I believe you have your leather whip with the lead tips in your saddle bags? If so, after the witch is tied to a tree, I want you to whip her until her back is torn open, raw and bleeding. However, I believe that you have the skill to stop before she dies from this punishment?"

"Oh yes, My Lord. I can whip the witch to the point of death, and you can then inform me of what further punishment you have in mind?" replied Nikallernor.

"First, before you start, I want to question the witch. Bring her to me."

Two of the soldiers dragged me to the land owner, and he grabbed me by the throat. "You will pay dearly for cursing my son to death, vile creature," snarled the land owner.

"But Lord," I gasped, "your son almost killed me in his wild ride through the village. What I said was in anger and annoyance at his rudeness. I certainly did not say anything that would cause his death."

"So, witch, you do not show any remorse for your evil deed. All you give me is excuses." With that, the land owner, in a violent rage, threw me onto the ground. He then kicked me as hard as he could, and I screamed in agony.

"Soldiers, here is what you will do. You will pick this bitch up and transport her into the village and tie her to the whipping post. Then one of you will stand guard over her while the rest of you and my son's companions round up the villagers. I want them formed into a circle before Nikallernor does his work," ordered the land owner.

"I note that you have the head that you cut from my son's horse? You will take this to the village and mount it on a stake, ensuring the head is facing the witch. I intend that first thing in the morning, you will pile brushwood round the witch, and she will burn to death. The horse will be a constant reminder of why she is suffering this fate. It will be the last thing she sees before she is consumed by the flames. Make sure her bag of demonology is placed next to her before you pile up the brushwood. They will all burn together," instructed the land owner.

In vain, I protested my innocence as I was dragged over to one of the soldier's horses and lifted up so that I sat in front of him. He had to hold tightly on to me, as in my terror, I was quaking all over and would have fallen to the ground.

I was taken to the village and tied to the village whipping post by two of the soldiers, using strong pieces of rope fastened through thick, firmly secured iron rings at the top and bottom of the post. They then made two of the villagers hammer a thick wooden stake into the ground and mount the horse's head onto it so that it directly faced me.

Meanwhile, the other soldiers and the land owner's son's companions soon rounded up the villagers who had abandoned the market and fled to their homes.

CHAPTER 3

Death of a Witch and the Killing of an Emperor

The villagers looked unhappy and sullen as they stood in a ring around the whipping post on which I was tied to and the stake with the horse's head mounted on it. A lot of the villagers had greatly benefited from my healing and the advice I gave them. They also hated the land owner and his dead son whose excessive demands for land rent and taxes caused them to live in near poverty.

The land owner gave a loathsome speech about my guilt and the punishment to be meted out to me, for my hand in the death of his son. He then ordered Nikallernor to ready his whip, a strong lengthy leather item with a lead tip securely fastened to the end, and one of the soldiers tore the clothes from my back. Then the whipping then began; the pain was excruciating, and I screamed out in agony. The whip tore into my back, ripping out chunks of bloody flesh with each blow. Soon my back was red raw, and the blood streamed down my body. A couple of times, I passed out and was revived by a bucket of icy water.

At last, the land owner cried out, "Enough. I can see that you love your work, Nikallernor, but as I ordered, I want the witch to live so she can enjoy the flames tomorrow."

The land owner then appointed two of the soldiers to guard me and instructed four of the others to relieve them, in teams of two, after the sand had run down from the top to the bottom of his inverted sandglass (approximately four hours in duration). He and the remaining soldiers and the dead son's companions then sought board and lodgings at the village inn.

I suffered endless agony during the night, and the thought of having to face a terrible death by fire the next morning many times made me wish that I had died under the lash. However, as fatigue was starting to set in and the first two guards had just been relieved by two of their companions, there was a movement behind me. The two guards, on full alert, issued a challenge.

The beautiful daughter of one of the villagers stepped out of the gloom, and they stiffened when they saw her face was covered with a dark hood. Despite her covered face, I recognized the maiden as one of the persons I had saved from the plague with my medicines. She was holding a tray containing a jug and two mugs. She held the tray out and said in a sweet voice, "I am sure that you both must be in need of a drink after being denied this with your being the nominated first change of guard?"

The two soldiers relaxed and grinned broadly, and each took a mug from the tray and filled it up with the liquid from the jug. They then took a large swig of the liquid and gave a sigh of satisfaction when the rich red wine hit the back of their throats.

"Tell me, maiden, why do you have your face covered?" inquired one of the soldiers suspiciously.

"Well, sir, if your captain—or any of your comrades—saw me, I would say I am going to a secret liaison with my lover from the village and did not want to be recognized," the maiden replied.

The guards appeared to be satisfied with this response and refilled their mugs. Very soon, all the wine was gone, and the maiden departed with the tray containing the empty jug and mugs. She winked at me as she passed the whipping post.

It was not long before the two soldiers were sleeping soundly, and then I heard a sudden movement behind me. A voice whispered, "Be very quiet, you must be as silent as possible while I release you."

My ropes were quickly cut, and I looked into the face of the father of the maiden who had brought the drinks for the soldiers. "I owe you so much for saving my daughter's life, and I am glad that I at last have the opportunity to repay you," said the villager. "In addition, it is also satisfying that I can thwart the plans of the hated land owner—in part, repayment for the oppression of our people."

I thanked him for coming to my rescue in my direst hour of need. However, he urged me to steel myself for an immediate journey as we had to travel as far away from the village as was possible before the next change of guard.

I was lifted onto his horse by the villager's son who was named Barsoniacus and who had emerged from the shadows. The villager, whose name was Aristophies, set off at a brisk pace. He was closely followed by his son on his own horse, to which he had fastened my bag.

Aristophies informed me that the drink given to the guards was heavily drugged, and the horses that were being used to enable my escape were borrowed from the livery stables whose owner was his cousin. He had to return the horses by dawn to ensure they were not missed.

We eventually entered the forest, and Aristophies assured me that he knew his way through every part of the woods and we would not become lost. Eventually, by means of a series of secret paths, we reached the clearing containing this hut and Barsoniacus sought out a torch and lit it from a flint in the hut. They then brought a ladder into the hut, cleared away the pine fronds on the hut floor, and lifted a trapdoor.

"Sorry," Aristophies said, "but you will have wait down there and not emerge until the land owner's soldiers and his son's companions stop looking for you. You will then probably have to live in this hut for a very long time. However, we will come back when it is considered safe and lift you out of the basement of the hut. We will put the food we brought into the basement, and this should keep you alive until we return. Is there anything else we can do before we leave?"

I asked him to go into my bag, which his son had brought, and to take out the healing ointment in the container he found in there and rub this into where my flesh had been torn off by the whip. He did this straight away and the pain was incredible and I was in absolute agony but as the pain subsided, relief temporarily flooded through my body. He then lowered me, my bag, and the food holder into the basement, closed the trapdoor, and ensured there were plenty of fresh fir fronds placed over the floor.

I heard Aristophies urge his son to move quickly, to ensure they were able to return the horses by dawn. I was later informed that they made it back to the village some time before sunrise and the changing of the guard.

When the change of guards arrived, they found the current two soldiers still soundly sleeping. They were woken up and said that the witch had cast a spell on them and paralyzed them before putting them to sleep. While still paralyzed, and before they fell asleep, they said that the witch summoned her demons, and they cut her bonds. The demons then lifted her up by her arms and flew away, carrying the witch to freedom.

The land owner was skeptical about the soldiers' story and ensured the village was checked to see if anyone was missing. When he found everyone was accounted for, he ensured the livery stable was checked and that all horses that should be there were present. Fortunately, the horses had cooled down by then, and after a thorough cleaning and brushing down, no one could tell they had been out of the livery stable during the night.

The land owner drew the leader of his soldiers aside and said, "Charistocles, I want you to take all of the soldiers and my late son's companions and search every part of the forest. I do not believe the two guards' story, and I think that the witch was somehow assisted by the villagers in her escape and that the two soldiers had been secretly drinking and had fallen asleep. So search the woods until the witch is found and torture the truth out of her. If any of the villagers were involved in her escape, they will be severely punished, and the two guards will wish they had never been born."

The forest was searched until I thought it would never end. I knew that despite the agonizing pain from the whipping, which many times almost forced me to cry out, I had to remain as silent as possible. How I wished I had more of the healing ointment and someone to administer it to me. The hut was entered at least five times, and I held my breath as they searched every part of the hut. However, no one thought to search the floor until the fifth search, and I trembled when one of the soldiers suggested searching the floor for any sign of a trapdoor.

They were just about to start the search when there was a loud shout. Another soldier rushed into the hut and said to his companions, "Quick, come with me, we are abandoning the search. Our troop leader has sent me to bring you back to where I left him. Elponista is dead, the ground collapsed under him, and he fell into a pit of sharply pointed upright stakes at the bottom. We have searched every part of the forest over and over again and found no sign of the witch. She has obviously been eaten by wild animals"

I heard one of the soldiers who had been searching my hut say, "We were in the process of searching for a hidden trapdoor to a basement of the hut when you came."

The soldier who had just arrived said derisively, "What! Did the old woman magically dig a basement cellar, and was she carried down there by her demons? I do not think so. Our troop leader will be waiting for us, and it is some distance from where we are standing, and he has a nasty temper if kept waiting too long, particularly after Elponista's death. So quickly, let us move along and leave the witch and her demons in the basement."

Fortunately, the searchers then moved on, and I never heard of them again. It was then just a patient wait until Aristophies and his son returned and hoisted me out of the basement.

When they came, they brought more food and informed me that the search was now over. However, I could never return to the village and would have to fend for myself in the forest. Fortunately, my knowledge of the various plants and herbs meant that I could look after myself and certainly would not starve. Especially as Aristophies showed me how to make and set rabbit snares.

* * *

"So that is my story, and you know all the facts," said the woman.

"Well, I am now very weary after the day's events, so I intend to go to sleep. However, in case you have any notion about escaping during the night, I am going to tie a strong cord around your waist, witch, and the other end will be fastened to my wrist. In case you are wondering, my profession has given me a built-in ability to wake at the slightest sound, no matter how deep my sleep," warned the chief assassin.

The old woman responded, "Why would I try to escape? I have nowhere to go, and I move so slowly. I would be easy prey for the savage animals that roam these woods at night."

The next morning, the old woman was untied, and they each ate until they had finished the remaining contents of the cooking pot, which they downed with the assistance of water drawn from the well outside the hut. When they had completed their meal, Damos said menacingly, "Well, student of the occult, you will now show us how to escape this accursed forest and make our way to the dockside if you know what is good for you!"

"Very well, sir, I have parchment and a quill pen and ink and will draw you a map. Even though I know it is your intention to kill me, despite what I say," responded the old woman.

When the map was completed, Damos closely inspected it and confirmed he could find his way out of the forest. He then drew his sword and said, "We appreciate your hospitality, old woman, but just in case Baron Nilanova's wife's soldiers come this way, in their extensive search for us, I must kill you to prevent you from giving us away."

The old woman cried out, "I am a student of the occult with considerable powers, and I know my time is near. However, despite this, if you kill me—after all the assistance I have rendered you—then I curse you and each of your companions. You will all be dead before your assignment is concluded, and your spirits will descend into the deepest depths of hell and be subject to the most excruciating torment."

"Old woman, many people in the past have cursed me, and I still survive. I will take my chances," retorted Damos. As he was saying this, he drew his sword, and in one fluid movement, he sliced off the old woman's head. He stuffed the map in into his belt and turned to his companions. "Come on, we've wasted enough time here, let's move on and see if we can get to the wharf before dark."

The three assassins soon arrived at the wharf side with the aid of the old woman's map. They found a safe place to hide and examined the royal galley, sleek in shape and resplendent in its deep blue and gold trimmings. The sharp pointed prow stood erect and proud, appearing eager to charge forward, as though to guide the vessel to its chosen destination. The curve of the back added to the overall aesthetic quality; indeed it was a splendid vessel. It was cleverly fitted out to cater for its royal and other aristocratic passengers and provide the maximum comfort, while ensuring the oarsmen had sufficient space for their rowing.

Damos looked closely at the five soldiers guarding the vessel and said to his companions, "The soldiers look very professional, so we need to be at our best to nullify them. We must be particularly quiet as we kill them, in case we alert any of the soldiers guarding the emperor's family in the nearby house. In that shed, over near the wharf's frontage is the oil which we need to commence the burning process of the galley. It is in large urns. Next to the urns are the torches we need to light to set off the oil and other inflammable material on the boat. When we have taken care of the soldiers after dark, just be casual and make your way over to the shed. I'll unlock it, and we'll select the quantity of material we need, take it over to the vessel, and carry out the burning process."

"Do not worry about the loss of Hernagos. If you do your jobs, then the royal galley is doomed, and we will have fulfilled our mission. Then we wait, collect our gold, and be on our way. We'll split Hernagos's gold equally between us," exclaimed Damos.

The three assassins hid in the nearby bushes and made themselves comfortable, while they waited for darkness to fall. They did not have long to wait before the royal palanquin arrived. It was a fully covered litter, with gold curtains and blue and gold trappings. It was carried by six slaves shouldering thick poles. The palanquin was accompanied by a troop of twelve soldiers in their military uniforms.

The palanquin was set down on its short wooden legs, and the very obese emperor was assisted—with considerable effort on the part of two of the slaves—to embark from it. He was followed by his two teenage sons, and they were all greeted by the person responsible for the maintenance of the house.

The house was a large rectangular structure, built around an inner open air courtyard. It was constructed of white granite and looked quite imposing at the edge of the forest.

The head of the house inquired, "I understood that you were to be accompanied by the empress and her son, Majesty?"

The emperor, with a disgusted look on his face, replied, "Her sickly young son is feverish again. He always seems to be ill—a disgrace to the royal family. So she is staying home at the palace to look after him. She fusses over that boy something chronic."

"I am sorry to hear that the empress is not here, and I hope the health of her son soon improves. Anyway, the royal galley is fully prepared, and we have the extra slaves to support the ones that you brought with you. Your accommodation in the house is also ready, and I believe you will enjoy the food and drink. I have arranged for you to leave reasonably early in the morning on the royal barge," remarked the head of the household.

"Good, I am sure you will have undertaken your duties in your customary efficient manner. You will also ensure when the people I have invited to the island arrive here, sometime tomorrow afternoon, that they are transported in the order I have specified? It will probably be after dark when the last of the guests arrive at Pleasure Island, and by then I may be too weary to welcome them. So I will send the captain of my guard to greet them, being the lowest in the pecking order, they can hardly complain if I am not there in person," instructed the emperor.

"It will be as Your Majesty orders. Would you now like to enter the house and settle in and enjoy some refreshments?' inquired the head of the household.

They went through the beautifully carved, though heavily bound, brass door and were led into a well-lit room with rich floor coverings and impressive wall murals and tapestries. There was a beautiful table of rare wood and accompanying chairs. The table was loaded with a wide selection of the emperor's favorite food and wines. The emperor's greedy face lit up, and he dived into the food without waiting to be served.

The feasting went on until the early hours with a wide variety of food and drink and continuous entertainment. There were musicians, gifted dancers, jugglers, and magicians—the latter with a variety of tricks to keep the audience enthralled. And then at last, the drunken emperor and his sons staggered off to their beds.

Meanwhile, the three assassins waited impatiently in their hidden location and considered their options before making their move. They carefully watched the galley guards and considered the best approach to gain an advantage over them. The guards each wore short tunics and carried a hoplite shield, bearing the royal crest, and they had a sword hanging from a belt at their side.

The assassins finally decided to make their move and silently made their way toward the royal galley and each crept up behind a guard, grabbed him in a powerful body hold, and slit his throat. However, one of the remaining three guards turned to address one of his slain companions and shouted out and drew his sword when he saw the assassins. The other guards also drew their weapons, and a fierce sword fight ensued.

Eventually, the guards were overcome and killed but not before one of the assassins received a deep sword thrust to his stomach.

The remaining two assassins carried their wounded comrade to the storage hut and laid him down at the side, away from the house and galley.

"We will have to work like dogs to burn the galley, now that Leonardos is badly wounded," Damos said to his companion. "I'll unlock the hut, and we'll carry the urns containing the oil to the galley."

The assassins worked as fast as they could, and eventually, all the urns and torches were next to the galley. Damos boarded the galley and his companion passed the urns and torches to him. The assassin then jumped onto the galley, and he and his leader poured the oil onto key areas of the galley. Once the oil was spread, Damos lit the torches, and he and his companion set fire to the various points where they had placed the oil and then jumped onto the wharf. The fire quickly took hold, and soon, the wooden galley was burning furiously.

The two assassins retreated to the side of the house and waited. Suddenly, the slave, who had been covertly placed in the household by arrangement of Baron Lysandros, shouted out loud and pointed to the galley. There was frantic movement as the slaves and other people in the household rushed over to the where the galley was moored. Soon there was only the emperor, his two sons, and the four royal guards in the house.

The slave who had raised the warning informed the two assassins that the house was empty, apart from the royal contingent. He also pointed out that the empress and her son had not traveled with the other members of the royal family and had stayed behind in the in the palace.

The two assassins then silently followed the slave into the building. The slave was instructed to tell the royal guards that the presence of two of them was required at the site of the fire by the head of the household.

It was with considerable reluctance that two of the royal guards left their posts, but they trusted the slave who was a favorite of the head of the household. When the two guards commenced to leave the building, the two assassins—waiting in the shadows— dispatched them with their swords. They then raced up to the remaining two guards who had had been watching their companions fall. Hence being alerted, both guards had time to draw their weapons and a fierce sword fight ensued. Eventually, however, the two assassins prevailed and the remaining guards were dead.

The assassins crept into the first royal bedroom and found the emperor sleeping soundly in his drunken stupor; hence he did not hear the commotion in the passageway. The chief assassin plunged his sword deep into the emperor's chest, and the assassins moved into the bedroom of the emperor's two sons.

Once again, they found the two princes sound asleep, and each assassin selected a prince and sank their respective swords into their bodies. Satisfied that all members of the royal family were dead, the two assassins made their way out of the house.

However, as the assassins headed for the forest, the slave who had facilitated their entry into the royal household—to cover his treachery—yelled out to the rest of the household who were watching the royal galley burn. He pointed to the escaping assassins and cried out, "Murderers, they have killed the royal family! Stop them!"

The assassins hesitated. However, when the remaining soldiers raced toward them, they hurried on. When they reached the trees, they were suddenly confronted with another group of soldiers.

"Do not worry, we were sent to meet you by Baron Lysandros. Your wounded friend is with us," said the soldiers' troop leader.

The chief assassin looked around and, by the flaming torchlight, perceived his wounded companion lying under a tree. He peered closely at the injured assassin and noted the wounds on his body.

"Our companion not only looks dead but appears to have a large hole in his chest, not unlike a spear wound?" retorted the suspicious Damos.

"Just give us our due reward, and we will mount the horses you brought, and we will be on our way. We will leave our dead companion to be attended to by you."

The troop leader nodded to the two soldiers standing behind the two assassins, and they plunged their swords into the assassin's backs. Each assassin screamed with pain and writhed in agony when they dropped to the floor of the forest, and they soon died. The troop leader looked contemptuously at the dead body of the chief assassin and retorted. "See, you now have your reward. I hope that you are satisfied—and you don't even need a horse to travel to where you are going."

This retort caused quite a lot of hilarity amongst the rest of the soldiers, and they laughed derisively. The soldiers pursuing the assassins burst through the trees as they were laughing.

CHAPTER 4

A Journey through Hell and the Prince's Escape

When the life force left his body, the chief assassin found himself floating freely through the air. He looked down and saw his corpse lying on the ground, in an ever-increasing pool of blood. Both of his arms were suddenly clasped in a grip of iron. He found himself descending at an incredible rate down a black tunnel and arrived with a bump at the bottom.

Glancing to his right and left, he was confronted with the most hideous beings he had ever seen. They were undoubtedly demons and a terrible sight to behold. They were black as night, covered in slimy, oily scales, with the most terrible countenance. And each stood on cloven hooves. It dawned on him that he really was in the deepest depths of hell and the demons were an exact description of those given to him in the story related by the old woman who had cursed him.

Suddenly, he heard the most horrible cackling and derisive laughter. Then his ears picked up a mocking voice. "You did not believe me when I said that I had placed a curse on you. Yes, you are now in the deepest depths of hell. Enjoy your time in purgatory." The mocking laugh then slowly faded into the background.

He found that his arms were free; however, he noticed that each demon carried a trident and were just behind him. They prodded him in the back, and the pain was excruciating.

He stumbled forward and, as he did so, saw that he was in a huge cavern. There was an almost-unbearable sulfurous stench permeating the whole of the area, which was lit by a fire, emanating from a pit in the center. Huge flames danced along the periphery of the pit, reaching hungrily toward the roof of the cavern. Suddenly, around the walls, a huge picture of people, obviously in absolute torment, was displayed. Loud moaning and screams for help came from the lips of their horribly contorted faces, and they held out their arms in helpless supplication.

The two demons prodded him toward the pit, and his heart sank as he noticed a multitude of reptilian figures with huge black wings, continually circling over the top of the pit. They had long lizardlike bodies and fierce dog's heads. Saliva dropped continuously from their huge jaws into the pit.

The chief assassin hesitated and felt both tridents forcibly rammed into his back and agonizing pain shot right through his whole being. Involuntarily, he screamed out in his absolute pain and agony. He soon found himself at the edge of the pit. Peering into the pit, he saw that the flames were shooting up out of a channel, which was situated part way up the wall and which circled the circumference of the pit. The channel appeared to contain a foul-smelling, slimy, oil-textured liquid. He saw dozens of figures, moving in a zombielike manner from the channel to a well in the center of the pit.

Once again, the chief assassin was subject to agonizing prods from the demons' tridents, and he found himself falling into the pit. He dropped into the foul-smelling, slimy, oil-textured liquid which covered the whole floor of the pit up to the level of the waist. He fell face first into the liquid, and it covered the whole of his body, and he felt it rush through his open mouth until he could swallow no more. A feeling of total nausea swept through him, and he felt as if his chest would explode. He wanted to throw up, but he was unable to do this, even though the foul smell and taste of the liquid was almost unbearable.

Suddenly, he found a semicircular-shaped baling pan in his hand with a long wooden handle. The pan was similar in size and design to those carried by the other figures in the pit. He found that he was drawn, like iron filings to a magnet, to the side of the pit. He noticed that each of the figures inside the pit filled their baling pans from the liquid. They then staggered over to the well and emptied the baling pan contents into the well. As soon as the baling pan was empty, each of the individuals struggled back to the channel, and the process was repeated.

The chief assassin stood watching this procedure until suddenly he felt two bolts of energy charge agonizingly through his body, and he looked up and saw that the two demons, standing at the edge of the pit, were pointing their tridents at him. Then another two bolts of energy shot out from the ends of the tridents and entered his body. He realized that to stop this torment, he had to commence the bale-filling and emptying procedure. Hence he filled his baling pan but found the weight of the liquid so great that he could hardly carry it, so he emptied a good portion of it out. However, as soon as he had partially emptied the pan, bolts of energy from the demons' tridents again charged agonizingly through his body. So he quickly refilled the baling pan and moved toward the well.

Huge flames were roaring up around the circumference of the pit, but yet as he filled the baling pan, he could feel no heat. So he thrust his hand into the center of the flames, and a terrible pain shot through him, and he screamed in agony as his hand blistered and burnt away. He quickly pulled the blackened stump of his arm away from the flames, and holding it with his uninjured hand, he looked unbelievingly at it while intense pain shot through him in agonizing waves.

Suddenly his hand started to form again and was soon restored to its former state, looking as though it had never been burnt. However, the terrible pain still persisted and did so for what seemed an eternity until it finally stopped. He hardly had time to recover from this before the bolts of energy from the demons' tridents once again rammed into his body.

Included in the terrible things he was experiencing in the pit were large fish in the liquid with huge piranhalike jaws and teeth. The savage fish bit into his limbs as he moved toward the well, tearing out huge lumps of flesh. Once again, the pain was agonizing, but there was no blood, and the flesh was quickly replaced. The terrible pain caused him to almost drop the baling pan, and most of the contents were spilt. As soon as this happened, the demons once again fired bolts of energy into his body, and this was kept up until he had gone back to the channel and refilled the baling pan.

At each step, the large fish kept tearing lumps of flesh from his body. He also found as he traveled back and forward from the channel to the well that the saliva from the dog-headed, lizardlike creatures circling the pit fell on him and burnt like acid with a corresponding pain as terrible as the bolts of energy from the demons' tridents.

He also noticed that no matter how much liquid was removed from the channel, the level remained the same. There was also no rest. The moment he stopped working, the bolts of energy from the demons' tridents once again charged agonizingly through his body, and the attacks by the fish intensified.

He moved on and looked around for his fellow assassins; they were all in the pit, but no matter how hard he tried, he could not reach them. When he cried out to them, it appeared that they were unable to hear him. This was the final straw, and the chief assassin's spirit finally broke, and he stopped and cried out in absolute despair. "How long must I put up with this torture?"

However, there was no one to hear him, and in the following silence, he felt the demons' agonizing bolts of energy course through his body, and the fish tore away at his flesh.

* * *

Meanwhile, back at the scene of the emperor's assassination, the soldier leading the group following the assassins stopped and glared suspiciously at the baron's men. He harshly inquired, "What are you men doing here?"

The head of the baron's troop replied, "Through one of his spies, the baron learned that there was a plot to assassinate the royal family and sent us to warn you. As we rode up, we perceived the first of these men lying in wait, and after he resisted, we killed him and then his two companions burst through the trees, obviously to meet up with him. They refused to surrender their arms, so we had no option but to kill them as well. You can see the three horses on which they were to escape are tethered over there."

One of the soldiers from the group chasing the assassins, upon seeing the dead bodies, suddenly cried out, "These are the men I saw riding away from the tavern after I had recovered from being drugged and I dashed into the street. They were responsible for the murders of Baron Nikon and his sons. They are scum and deserved to die."

The soldier leading the group, however, said, "It is good that they are dead, but surely it would be better if they were still alive so we could torture them and learn who was paying their blood money. It must be someone very powerful with a vested interest in seeing the emperor and his family dead. It is indeed fortunate that the empress's son was so ill that they did not attend."

"What! The empress and her son are still alive?" responded the baron's troop leader.

The leader of the soldiers threw a suspicious look in the direction of the troop leader. "You do not look too pleased about that. Did the baron have a hand in the plot to assassinate the royal family?"

"Why, of course not. It is great news about the empress and her son, and the baron will be delighted when he hears that they escaped the royal family's assassination," responded the troop leader. "We must return at once to the baron's castle and inform him. He is still under house detention, although he and his wife and some of the castle staff suffered only minor fevers and certainly did not have the plague. They are now all back to full health. When the baron was informed by one of his spies that there was a plot to assassinate the royal family, we left the castle in secret, in an attempt to foil the assassination, but we were too late in arriving here."

"Very well. We will sort everything out here. The baron can inform the empress of the emperor's and the princes' deaths and ensure she is properly looked after," said the soldier.

The troop leader saluted, and he and the rest of his soldiers mounted their horses and set off at a fast pace for the baron's castle. When they reached the baron's hunting lodge, the soldiers dismounted and led their horses into the livery stable. The slaves responsible for the upkeep of the lodge made sure the horses were properly rubbed down, fed, and watered.

The soldiers then made their way through the forest until they reached the camouflaged entrance to the secret passage to the baron's castle. They lit a torch taken from a holder in the wall of the passageway and made their way, along the passage, until they reached the door into the castle dungeons.

Using a large key, previously given to him by the baron, the troop leader opened the strong wooden, brass-bound door, and the soldiers filed into the dungeon. The troop leader closed and locked the door behind him, and the soldiers made their way up to the main part of the castle.

While the rest of the soldiers settled into their quarters, the troop leader sought out the Baron. "My Lord, the emperor and his two sons are dead, and they will shortly rest with their mother who died of the plague in the royal crypt. I have left the bodies of the assassins, apart from one who died in the forest with the remainder of the emperor's soldiers. I made sure that the three remaining assassins were killed before the emperor's soldiers reached us in the forest," reported the troop leader. "Unfortunately, the empress elected to stay behind at the palace, as her young son was sick, and she wanted to personally attend to his needs."

"It is good that the empress was not in attendance with the rest of the royal family when they were assassinated, we can turn this fact to our advantage. You will go to the front gate and inform the besieging soldiers there that plague conditions do not exist in the castle. It was a false alarm. However, make sure that one of our soldiers leaves by the secret passage before then and bursts in on the besieging soldiers, just as you are finished talking. He can tell the leader of the soldiers that he has come straight from the wharf side and that the emperor and his two sons are dead. You can then offer our services and say it is imperative that the besieging soldiers rush to protect the empress against any further assassination attempts," ordered the baron.

"I will do as you have instructed, My Lord," replied the troop leader. He then hurried away to carry out the baron's orders. He briefed one of the soldiers and made his way to the castle gate. He was delighted to see that following his presentation and the news from the soldier who had left by the secret passage, that the besieging soldiers did not hesitate and mounted their horses and raced off in the direction of the royal palace.

The empress was in her chambers when her personal aide burst in to see her. It was elegantly furnished, with richly covered couches and beautifully carved chairs and tables made of the finest wood. The tapestries depicted breathtaking scenes of the royal garden and richly dressed people moving elegantly through it. There were frescoes, depicting the royal barge, scooting along under the straining oars of the hardworking galley slaves and of parties, with people enjoying all kinds of wine and rich food.

Bowing low, the aide said, "Your highness, the Baron Lysandros is here with his soldiers, offering his support after the slaying of the emperor and his two sons. He has linked up with the soldiers who returned after guarding his castle."

"He is quick off the mark. I've only just received news of the emperor's death myself. Despite his so-called good intentions, I do not trust him. He is power hungry, and I fear he means my son and I harm. He maintained from the moment I married the emperor, that the daughter of a mine owner from some remote part of Atlantis, was not an appropriate match for the ruler of this country," responded the empress. "Despite this, I suppose you had better show him in. However, before then, see the captain of my guard and tell him that I need to see him straight after the baron has left my chambers."

The aide bowed and left the chambers and scurried off to brief the captain of the empress's guard.

The baron was then shown into the empress's presence by her aide. He bowed and said, "I have come to offer my services to Your Highness, following the slaying of the emperor and the two princes. I suppose you have heard that it was my soldiers that killed those murderess assassins? It is indeed fortunate that you and your son were not in attendance when the royal party was assassinated."

"Yes, indeed, My Lord. But I have my aide to advise me and my trusted captain and his guards to protect me should there be any further assassination attempts. The captain is a brave and skilled warrior with a cool head and is highly intelligent. Hence I consider that I am already in good hands," responded the empress.

"Very well, Your Highness. I have called a meeting of the council to discuss who could possibly be responsible for the emperor and the princes' slaying. It will be attended by all the noble lords who fortunately were unable to attend the planned soiree on Pleasure Island. Undoubtedly, you will have heard that the assassins destroyed the royal galley by fire to ensure the emperor and his entourage did not escape?" inquired the baron.

"Yes, I was fully briefed, but why have I not been invited to the meeting? I am, after all, now in charge of the country, following the death of my husband and two stepsons," inquired the empress.

"The council of nobles considers that until all the facts of the assassination are fully explored, you should not attend any of these meetings, Your Highness. However, I will fully appraise you of whatever comes out of the meeting as soon as it is concluded," responded the baron.

"Very well, I await your communication and hope that the meeting comes up with the answer as to why the emperor was assassinated, and I believe if this is done thoroughly, it will reveal by whom," said the empress.

The baron bowed and left the chamber.

As soon as he was out of sight, the captain of her guide entered the empress's chamber. He was a handsome man with finely chiseled features and wavy blond hair. He had a well-groomed beard, as was the habit of the noble males of Atlantis. The captain was tall and had broad shoulders. He looked every inch the fine warrior that he was, and his bearing demonstrated that he was recruited from one of the leading aristocratic families.

The empress did not mince words. "We are in great peril. The Baron Lysandros is a vicious, ruthless scoundrel. He has ambitions to be the new emperor, and I do not doubt that he was behind the assassinations and will stop at nothing to achieve his objectives. I am sure he will cunningly direct the meeting discussions to the fact that I made excuses not to attend the emperor's royal entourage's trip to Pleasure Island. He will use this to implicate me in the emperor's assassination and will say that, as captain of my guard, you must have been involved in my plotting. Hence it will only be a matter of time before we and all people close to me are arrested, publically denounced, and executed. He will then make sure the prince has a nasty accident to leave the way open for him to ascend the throne and declare himself emperor.

"I know we have not had the most tranquil of relationships, captain. However, I am aware that you are a man of honor, loyal to the throne of Atlantis. Hence I appeal to you to escape and save my son so that one day he may take his rightful place as emperor of Atlantis. You can escape by the secret passage and see Karpella, the livery station manager who resides in the auxiliary livery stables, outside the royal palace. I have asked him to prepare for such a day as this, and he will ensure that you and my son have fine, fresh horses to facilitate your escape. Do this Captain Arkella, and I will be in your debt forever.

"However, before you go, take this letter I have prepared and make sure you give it to my son. He should hand it to the old man you seek out, named the Monitor. You will find him living in the Charis mountain range. I believe you are familiar with that area?" inquired the empress.

"I do know that mountain range very well as I trained in that area as a young soldier. I also love to fish and hunt there. It is a beautiful region. There are rumors that the Monitor lives close by, but I have never glimpsed him. However, I would prefer to stay and fight with Your Highness. Surely, together we can defeat the Baron and foil his evil plans?" responded the captain.

"The baron has obviously laid his plans very carefully and will have bribed and threatened key council members. Hence I believe that no one will be prepared to stand up against him. So you must escape to ensure my son's safety," responded the empress. "I will stay and try to do everything I can to cover your escape. You must take your weapons and the minimum of clothing for you and my son and go. The livery station manager, as well as fresh and reliable horses, will give you some food and drink for your journey. I know you will do everything you can to ensure the safety of my son, and I want you to tell him how much I love him and that one day I hope to see him again. I dare not expend time to see him before he leaves, as the baron will have his spies watching my every move."

The captain bowed and reluctantly left the empress. He then collected the young prince—a pale-faced, sickly-looking boy of some ten years of age. He was tall for his years, but painfully thin and looked as though he would break in half under the slightest wind pressure. The packing was quickly done, and the clothes they were taking were thrown into a couple of animal-skin bags.

Captain Arkella took the lead, carrying the bags of clothes, and after he left them with the livery station manager, he returned via the secret tunnel to the palace, for his weapons. These consisted of a bow and arrows, shield, and a long spear. He wore his sword in a scabbard in his belt.

They loaded the horses, with the most belongings placed on the prince's horse. The captain then collected the bags of food and the drink, and he and prince mounted the horses and set off at a brisk pace. Fortunately, the auxiliary livery stable, like the exit from the secret tunnel, was hidden by trees; hence they could not be detected by the palace guards.

Meanwhile, the meeting conducted by the baron was concluded. It was agreed that the empress, the captain of her guard, and those people close to her would be arrested. They would be charged with high treason and murder for organizing the assassination of the royal family. The baron would be given protective custody over the prince and be responsible not only for his safety but for training him to be the future emperor of Atlantis.

The baron headed straight to the empress's chamber after the council meeting finished. He burst into the chamber, followed by a detachment of his soldiers.

"Where is your brat, Empress, and that favorite of yours, the captain of your guard?" asked the baron with a sneering look on his face.

"What right do you have to burst unannounced into my chambers? When you come into my presence, you are also required to bow and address me by my title, which is *Your Highness*, and you certainly have no right to display disrespect to the prince. So leave here straight away before I have you and your soldiers arrested," exclaimed the outraged empress.

The grandstanding Baron bowed in a mock gesture and responded, "By the power vested in me by the royal council, would Your Royal Highness please make herself available for arrest for high treason and inform me where the royal prince and the captain of your guard can be found?"

Seeing this, the baron's soldiers howled with laughter. Her face purple with rage, the tight-lipped empress replied, "All right, so you are going to arrest me, but what will happen to my son?"

The baron, in a sarcastic voice, said, "Oh, do not concern yourself about your son. I will personally take good care of him!"

When the soldiers heard this, their hilarity was unbounded. "Well, where is your son and the captain of your guard?" demanded the baron in an aggressive manner.

"You're so clever, you find them," responded the empress.

The baron turned to his soldiers and snarled, "Search the palace. If necessary, turn it upside down, but find that brat of a boy and the captain of the guard."

Eventually, they gave up the search and reported back to the baron. He kicked the furniture in the empress's chamber in frustration. "The boy and the captain have somehow escaped from the palace. Does anyone have any idea where they could be heading?"

"When I was a young soldier, Lord, I spent some time in a training camp 'round the Charis mountain area. The captain was also a soldier there, and on occasions, he returns there to go fishing and hunting. I believe that is where he is heading. He can hide in the mountains, and there is plenty of game in the forest, at the foot of the mountain range and fish in the crystal clear, free-flowing mountain streams," responded one of the soldiers.

"It sounds the perfect place for someone wanting to hide," replied the baron. "Then go quickly, prepare your selves for the hunt, and find me the prince and captain. If you have to kill them, I want you to bring their bodies back to the palace to show these fools of councilors that the prince is dead and that I am the only one fit to rule Atlantis. I will tell the councilors that the prince and captain were killed by bandits in the forest before you could reach them."

The soldiers quickly prepared themselves and soon were mounted and headed in a fast gallop toward the Charis mountain range.

* * *

Despite being aware that they would be pursued by the baron's soldiers, no matter how hard the captain tried to urge the prince on, it was difficult to maintain a fast pace. He continually exhorted the prince to greater efforts, but it was just beyond the capabilities of the sickly child. However, they kept going right through the night with the prince strapped on to his horse to prevent him falling off it with sheer exhaustion.

Eventually, they came within sight of a rich, green forest at the base of the Charis mountain range. The captain looked back and spotted the pursuing soldiers. He realized they could not outrun them. So he instructed the prince, "I want you to ride on, straight through the forest and toward the mountain range. You then should look for the man they call the Monitor and give him the letter I am now going to give you. He will take you with him and will look after you."

The prince looked at the captain and responded, "I do not want to leave you, and I am totally exhausted. Surely we can reach the forest, hide in there from our pursuers, and rest awhile? We will then be fresh to search for and find this Monitor together."

The captain pointed to the pursuing baron's soldiers and replied, "See those riders? They are Baron Lysandros's men, and they are determined to catch and kill us. So please, my little prince, summon some hidden courage and take heart and ride on. I will make my stand on the knoll just ahead and hold them back, as much as I am able to."

"I will do as you advise, Captain," responded the prince. "Tell me, will we ever see each other again?"

"It is highly unlikely in this life. However, it has been a pleasure to serve you, so please remember me and my family when you become emperor of Atlantis. You must now ride on and may the gods be with you and watch over you," said the captain.

CHAPTER 5

Heroic Last Stand and the Monitor's Refuge

Somehow the prince summoned up some hidden energy, and pumped with adrenalin, he set off at a fast pace toward the forest. Meanwhile, the captain mounted the knoll, carrying only his bow across his shoulders and a quiver of arrows at his back and his sword dangling at his side. The knoll was difficult to climb as it was comprised of crumbling limestone with outcrops of grass and weeds. However, the captain was superbly fit and a natural athlete and was able to negotiate his way to the top. He knew that to pass him, the pursuers had to ride through the gulley running alongside the knoll. Hence, they would be well within arrow's range. So he made ready his bow and arrows and waited for the soldiers to come within range.

The soldiers spurred their mounts on, knowing that their quarry was within their grasp. They saw the captain climb onto the knoll and the prince ride off, and they did not hesitate but came on at speed. However, when they were just out of arrow range, the leader of the soldiers held up his hand and stopped the pursuing soldiers.

"The terrain dictates that the only way we can go past the knoll and catch the prince is to traverse the gulley. We will hold our shields up so that they protect our bodies and move as quickly as we can through the gulley and take up position behind the captain. We can then pick him off at our leisure and then go after the brat of a boy."

It did not take long to ready their shields and the pursuers headed off for the gulley. They each wore helmets made of a single piece of bronze. This protected the face and back of the head and had openings for the soldier's eyes and mouth. The round shields offered protection to the upper body but made riding cumbersome. However, due to the fact that to lighten the horses for the pursuit, the soldiers were not wearing body armor, their shields did not protect the whole of their upper body and significant parts of their chest were exposed and were vulnerable to an expert archer.

Hence, the captain knew that the best way to kill or wound any of the soldiers was to aim his arrows so that they penetrated the unprotected spaces on their chests. A great advantage was that the riders were restricted by having to move relatively slowly in single file through the gulley. Knowing he had a great advantage, the captain, with adrenalin flowing, tensed with anticipation; and when the riders were within range, he fired off the first arrow. He was an excellent archer and had won many trophies with his ability with the bow. There was also only a slight breeze to take into consideration so his first arrow sped through, found its mark, and penetrated the lead rider's chest. He fell from his horse with a loud cry, but this did not deter the remaining riders who kept on coming.

However, when three more of the pursuers had been incapacitated, the remaining six turned tail and fled. The captain then sent a well-aimed arrow into the back of the rider at the rear of the fleeing soldiers.

The pursuers regrouped and realized that two of the remaining five soldiers were also expert archers; so the five soldiers advanced slowly toward the captain's position, using their shields as protection. When they were within range, the two bowmen fired continuous arrows at the captain. Eventually a direct hit brought the captain tumbling down from the knoll but not before one of his arrows had passed through the throat of one of the bowmen, killing him.

One of the soldiers walked up to the bottom of the knoll and drove his sword deep into the captain's body, "That's for killing my comrades, one of whom was my brother." He turned to his companions and snarled, "I'm sick of this place; let's move on and catch up with the brat."

However, the other three soldiers shuffled uncomfortably, and at last one of them spoke. "The prince is nowhere in sight and has obviously entered the forest. It is full of wild animals and bandits, and without the captain to look after him, he will undoubtedly perish. There are also now only four of us; how will we fend off an attack by well-armed bandits? We are totally exhausted and virtually starving; let us rest and eat and then we can go back and report to the baron that we have killed both the captain and the boy. We can bury our dead comrades and the captain's body under the many rocks there are around the knoll before we leave. We can then tell the baron that while we rested on top of the knoll, wild animals crept up and took and ate the bodies."

They all agreed that this was a good idea and climbed to the top of the knoll with their provisions. Very soon they had settled down and fallen asleep out of sheer exhaustion.

The next morning, the pursuers busied themselves burying the captain and the rest of the soldiers under the many rocks close to where they had dragged the bodies. They then ate their remaining food and set off to return to the royal palace.

Meanwhile, despite its tiredness, the prince's horse went at a fast gallop; and soon they entered the forest. It was a dark and forbidding place, and the cries and screams of the birds and animals added to the prince's terror. He fearfully urged his horse on and looked around him at the forest of green, praying that nothing would come out at him. He earnestly wished the captain was still with him and fell into a deep depression as he realized he was totally alone with no one to help him. The going was now particularly slow as the horse cautiously picked its way through the woods, following the almost invisible trail. Finally, the prince was overcome with exhaustion and fell asleep and would have fallen off the horse but for the strong ropes that bound him to it.

Finally they emerged from the forest, and the horse pulled up on a flat grassy clearing and contentedly munched the rich grass. It was totally exhausted and could go on no more, and meanwhile, the prince slept on.

While this was happening, the person known as the Monitor was making his way home after his overnight stay and the healing sessions he had undertaken at the nearby village. He was humming to himself in satisfaction as he sat on his trap and urged his horse along at a gentle pace. The Monitor was incredibly old with a full head of pure white, curly hair. His face revealed the hard life he had led, although for all his years, he was incredibly energetic and led an extremely active lifestyle. He wore a full-length tunic of a light silvery color made of some alien material, which covered his sparse frame down to his knees. The cloak he wore over the tunic was a light brown color and made of wool. He wore leather sandals on his feet which, like his cloak, had been secured from the villagers in payment for his healing services. The cloak had a hood which the Monitor had pulled over his head to protect his face from the still strong sun.

Suddenly the horse reared up when something appeared on the road before them. It was an image of the empress who said, "I have been imprisoned by Baron Lycus and the royal council, wrongly accused of murdering the emperor and his two sons. My son, the remaining royal prince, is being hunted down by the baron's soldiers even as you look at me now. If they catch him and the captain of my guard, who is accompanying him, they will undoubtedly kill them.

"Baron Lysandros will then seize the throne of Atlantis and declare himself emperor. I beg you as a favor to an old friend, who once saved your life, protect the prince and my captain from their enemies. I then ask you to give them shelter and raise the prince as one of your own. I know you can train and develop him so that he can grow up to respected manhood and one day take his rightful place as emperor of Atlantis.

"The prince has a letter from me to you to identify who he is. He also carries the royal crest as a tattoo on his chest; I have sketched the crest on the parchment comprising the letter.

"I used the compound you gave me to facilitate my appearance before you. You will no doubt have detected that I have taken the whole of the compound in one go? I have kept it since you gave it to me in a sachet on a chain round my neck. Fortunately, I was not searched prior to my imprisonment; one of the few privileges accorded to me as empress prior to my torture and subsequent death.

"You warned me that taking the compound all at the one time would kill me. However, I needed to take it all to ensure I would be able to deliver the whole message to you from my prison cell. Besides which, by dying, I will foil the evil baron's malicious plans. He was looking forward with eager anticipation to torturing me to death.

"So goodbye old friend; may the gods go with you." The empress's image then vanished.

The Monitor dismounted and settled his frightened horse down and said in a soothing voice, "Ajax, it was just a message from a sincere friend, who is in great trouble and who desperately needs our assistance." He then patted the horse and gave it a carrot.

The Monitor mounted the trap and coaxed the horse into action, "Come on, old fellow, we have a prince and the future of Atlantis to save."

They set off at a brisk pace and rapidly closed in on the forest. However, the darkness started to fall, and the Monitor became concerned that he would not be able to locate the person he was looking for in the woods. "I wish I had the prince's profile on record, and I could use the homing device in my disk and be confident of locating him," he said to himself.

However, he eventually came across the prince, sleeping soundly on his horse. The horse was munching contentedly on the thick, lush grass of the clearing at the edge of the forest.

"I'd better move quickly, young prince, to load you into the trap, secure your horse, and set off for home. The baron's soldiers will be hot on your trail, and I do not want to be caught out in the open. However, I wonder why you are not accompanied by the empress's captain of the guard?" mused the Monitor.

The Monitor untied the prince from the horse and gently lifted him into the trap. He secured the prince's horse to the rear of the trap, and they set off for the Monitor's home. This was in a cavern complex shrewdly hidden from the sight of the casual passerby, at the foot of the Charis mountain range.

When they reached the cavern complex, the Monitor took hold of a golden chain, which hung around his neck, and pressed what appeared to be a huge red crystal in the center of a large, round gold disk fastened to the chain. The front of the cliff side, which had appeared to be solid, suddenly revealed three openings. The openings were easily large enough to allow two people to enter plus the horses and the trap. They entered the middle cave, and once they were well inside, the Monitor again pressed the center of the disk and a solid front was again presented on the front of the cavern complex.

The Monitor called out, "Lights," and the cave was suddenly bathed in a strong light; he gently lifted the prince out of the trap and laid him on one of the beds in the cave. He then opened a gate to an offshoot of the main cavern and led Ajax and the trap and the prince's horse, through it. He untied the horses and watered and fed them before leaving the cavern and closing the gate behind him.

The Monitor lay down on an adjacent couch and was soon fast asleep. The next morning, he was wakened by the prince who was stroking and talking to his horse, which had its head over the cavern gate.

"I believe that you are named Evanistas? Well, from now on you will use the name Euthymios to protect your identity," said the Monitor to the prince. "Hence, you should quickly become accustomed to it, as it would appear you are fated to be here with me for a long time. Unfortunately, your mother is dead; but what happened to the captain of the empress's guard, who was accompanying you?"

The prince related what had happened, up to the time the captain elected to stay behind and hold off the baron's soldiers who were following them. He mentioned how the captain urged him to escape, to facilitate his meeting up with the Monitor.

"He was a brave man and undoubtedly died delaying the baron's soldiers; you owe him a debt of gratitude and can repay him by working hard to become a great emperor," responded the Monitor gravely. "Anyway, I am known as the Monitor; and while you are here, you can regard yourself as my student, and hence you will call me master. You will follow my directions without question. Remember that Baron Lysandros is now in charge of Atlantis, and should he learn that you are still alive, he will relentlessly hunt you down. In time, you will learn all the secrets of the cave; but remember you must keep everything you learn to yourself. The knowledge in here is very sensitive, as well as dangerous, and we must make sure it does not fall into the hands of those people who would use it for their own selfish ends."

The prince looked at the Monitor with innocent eyes. "I will do everything you ask of me, master; I know I will miss the royal palace, and already, my heart aches for my mother. One day, I swear that I will kill Baron Lysandros for what he has done to my family and the captain of my mother's guard."

"Bravely said, but first, I must feed you up to put some flesh on your bones; and we need to develop a plan for your training and development. Leave this with me for consideration, and I will let you know what I have in mind. However, first we must eat, for I am quite hungry; and you must be the same?' queried the Monitor.

The prince washed at the spring inside the cave and put on some fresh clothes. Meanwhile, the Monitor prepared a fulfilling meal consisting of a mixture of grain, vegetables, and goat meat and placed this on a table in the center of the cavern along with a pitcher of goat's milk. The hungry prince dived into the meal and drank thirstily from his earthenware cup of milk.

When he had finished, the Monitor inquired, "It appears you enjoyed your meal; are you feeling much better now?"

"Oh yes, master. The meal was delicious, but I have never seen some of the vegetables before that were on the plate; where do they and the rest of that beautiful food come from?" responded the prince.

"The milk and meat you enjoyed comes from the goats, which graze in a closed-in, hidden canyon in the mountains close by. The vegetables are grown by me, close to where the goats are kept along with olive and fig trees. You will note in time that some of the vegetables are different from anything else grown around here. This is because they have been raised from seed, taken from the vessel which I used to travel to the surface of this planet. However, they are very nutritious, and I am glad that you appeared to enjoy them as much as I do. The cereals as well as the flour and yeast extract for our bread and our shoes, clothing, and other manufactured items are in payment of the services I provide to the villagers and in exchange for the excess vegetables, figs, and olives. I make the best olive oil you will find for our cooking and for salad dressing. Our excess olive oil is also bartered with the villagers for any of our requirements or, like our other produce items, given to those villagers who are really in need."

The prince inquired, "The captain gave me a letter from my mother to give to you. So here it is; what message does it contain, master?"

The Monitor opened the bulky letter and some really beautiful and seemingly rare jewels fell out. He picked the jewels up and examined them very closely. He then opened the letter and carefully read it before speaking. "Your mother asks me to ensure you are comprehensively trained and fully developed so that one day, you may take your place as a highly respected emperor of Atlantis. The jewels are in payment for this and for my housing and feeding you. They apparently were wedding and other gifts to your mother from the emperor and the people of Atlantis. I will keep them safe, and when the time is ripe for you to go forth and fulfill your destiny, I will give them to you. People prize such things, and they will be very useful to you should you wish to use them as payment."

"They are yours, master; a gift from my mother to you. I cannot take them," responded the prince.

"You have a good heart, young prince, and I admire that and will not argue with you," said the Monitor. "I will ensure the jewels are kept safe until a later date. So tell me, before I show you around the cavern complex, is there anything else you want to know?"

The prince replied, "I would like to know how you met my mother?"

The Monitor responded, "It is an interesting story, how I met your mother. You see, one day I was making haste to go to the village, where they were plagued with a mysterious sickness. Unfortunately, my horse, which was very old, was having problems with his health. By the time I had given him the appropriate medication and associated treatment, I completely forgot to take my protective fluid to shield me from the sickness in the village.

"I was well on my way to the village when I realized this, but it was too late to turn back. So I carried on, entered the village, and treated the sick. When I was finished and had eaten and rested, I set off to return to the cave. I had taken the same medicine that I had given to the villagers, but it was not as effective with regard to my metabolism as my own fluid mixture. So I began to exhibit the same sickness that had affected the villagers. To add to my woes, my old horse gave his last breath and collapsed dead in front of my trap. I rushed to attend to him, and I suddenly felt dizzy and collapsed.

"Your mother, who was then ward of the landowner whose estate butted onto the area in which I live, passed close to my trap a short time later. She was out for a ride accompanied by six of her guards. Your mother, being adventurous, had deliberately strayed onto the neighboring land.

"'Quickly, Eutranius,' she said to one of her guards, 'see what is wrong with the man at the trap.'

"Eutranius replied, 'There has been a lot of sickness in the nearby village due to a mysterious malady which is rampant in this area. The man may be infected and could well pass the sickness on to us. I suggest my lady that we leave him to his fate.'

"'Nonsense,' replied your mother, 'we will take that chance. I want one of you to hitch your horse to his trap and gently lie the man down in the back, and we will drive him back to our estate, and I will treat the man myself.'

"Reluctantly, one of the soldiers freed my dead horse and hitched his mount to my trap. He then ensured I was laid out as comfortable as possible before climbing onto the trap and taking the horse's reins. At your mother's signal, he followed her and the soldiers to your grandfather's castle.

"I was feverish for several days before I made a complete recovery. Your mother was wonderful and made sure I was given the very best care.

"One day, when I was back to full health, she came and took me on a tour of the castle. It was typical of the buildings of the landowners of Atlantis, with walls of white granite quarried from the Charis mountains. The building was of rectangular structure with a flat roof, and it was built round a central courtyard.

"The interior of the castle contained well-decorated rooms with beautiful frescoes; tapestries showing landscapes, battle depictions, and seascapes; and there were also beautiful marble statues. There were the most wonderful woven carpets on the floor, all brightly colored and of exquisite patterns. There were separate living and dining areas and special bedrooms for the castle elite and also living, sleeping, and eating areas for the castle servants or slaves. The soldiers were quartered in a separate part of the castle.

"The castle consisted of two levels, and the upper floor was reached via a beautiful staircase with an elegantly carved handrail.

"There were bathrooms and a plethora of storerooms to ensure adequate food, wine, and other supplies to the household. The castle was entered by a strong wooden door bound with bronze. I saw many soldiers, whose role it was to guard the castle and keep its occupants safe.

"Your mother loved her garden, and it contained herbs of various kinds, which were used in the kitchen for cooking. In addition, she cultivated a diversity of colorful plants and beautiful flowering shrubs. There were also olive, fig, and a profusion of other fruit trees growing in the courtyard. The vegetables and other consumables to feed the castle inhabitants were obtained from the estate, which was quite large in area.

"The livery stables were in a corner of the building, and I had never before seen such beautiful horses. One in particular focused my attention, and I found it easy to use my animal communication skills to make contact with him. His head was over the stable door, and he obviously enjoyed the attention I was giving him.

"Your mother clapped her hands in delight. 'Ajax has never allowed anyone but me to stroke him like that; he obviously has taken a real liking to you. When you leave here, he is yours to use as a replacement for your dead animal.'

"I protested that I could not pay for her horse or repay the kindness she had shown me, and she would need Ajax. Your mother said that she was promised in marriage to your father, the emperor, who had recently lost his wife to the plague. She said that shortly, she would be leaving by palanquin (litter), carried by the castle slaves and would be accompanied by a troop of the castle's soldiers. Apparently, the emperor had some of the finest horses in the land, and she had been promised one of the best as a wedding gift. So she said it would considerably ease her mind if she knew Ajax was being well looked after.

"I asked if there was anything I could do for her in return for her kindness? She replied that she knew of my reputation as a healer and spiritual guide. She requested that if there was something that would assist her if she was in danger that would more than repay her.

"Her request was given considerable thought before I handed her a small sachet, which hung by a golden chain around my neck next to the gold disk. This contained a herb which, when taken in small doses in water and in conjunction with deep meditation, enabled a person's spirit to leave their body and astral travel. However, the distance a spirit can travel by an individual who is not used to this experience, is very limited. They must also ensure they completely focus on the person with whom they wish to communicate, who must be within range of their meditation skill capacity. It should be noted that the herb does not grow naturally anywhere on this planet. I cultivate a small amount of the herb in my garden in the mountains. So I ensured your mother was instructed in deep meditation concepts to ensure she could gain the required benefit from the use of the herb in time of need.

"The more advanced spiritual healers, like I am, by imbibing significantly more than the average person, can use this herb to communicate with people over a very wide area. However, as I informed your mother, if the whole of the sachet of herbs is imbibed by a person not used to taking it, after the communication is completed, they will surely perish. The internal organs will be systematically destroyed, and the individual concerned will suffer almost instant death. So unfortunately, your mother, by imbibing the whole of the sachet of herbs in order to facilitate our communication, is now no longer alive. It was a brave thing to do, but she did it out of love for you, young prince. So you must work hard to be a credit to her and honor her name."

The prince, choked with emotion, felt the hot tears run down his face. When he recovered his composure, he said, "I will work hard to be a credit to my mother; but when I become emperor, I will not forget what Baron Lysandros has done to my family, and he will pay dearly for his evil deeds."

* * *

Prior to the empress's taking the herb to facilitate astral travel, one of the baron's soldiers guarding her, opened the cell door. He dropped the tray containing a bowl of watery gruel and a goblet of water comprising her midday meal onto the seat next to where she was seated.

"Here is your repast, specially prepared for someone of your status, your majesty," the soldier declared in a mocking voice. "Enjoy your meal; you won't receive anything better."

The soldier then left the cell and walked away laughing loudly after locking the cell door. Once the soldier had gone, the empress removed the golden chain from around her neck and opened the sachet of herbs. She poured the whole contents of the sachet into the goblet of water and stirred the resulting liquid with the metal spoon provided for consuming the gruel.

When she was satisfied that the liquid was sufficiently stirred, she sat cross-legged on the floor of the cell and began to enter a state of deep meditation. She interrupted this exercise only to drink deeply from the goblet until all of its contents were imbibed. The empress then recommenced her deep meditation exercise and attained a state where she was able to contact the Monitor. She then undertook her communication with the Monitor, and when it was completed, she stretched out on the bench in the cell.

The empress did not have too long to wait before she experienced the first stabbing pain. This was excruciating, but as her internal organs rapidly went into massive meltdown, she quickly expired. Blood poured from every orifice of her body and ran across the bench and onto the floor.

One of the soldiers guarding the empress casually made his way to her cell to collect the tray which had contained her food. He opened the door and took one look at the bloody body and pools of blood on the floor and rushed out to collect the rest of the soldiers guarding that cell block.

When the baron was informed of the empress's death, he went ballistic. The thought that the empress had cheated him of the opportunity to totally humiliate her and make her suffer unimaginable pain as she was slowly put to death caused him to hammer the table with his fist in rage. In a fit of uncontrollable temper, he had every one of the cell block guards severely whipped and the guard who had brought the empress her food put to death.

Meanwhile, a sudden weariness overcame the Monitor with the emotional strain of relating the story of how he met the prince's mother and the concern about what to do for the best for the prince. He said in a soft voice, "But enough of our discussions for now, let us move on to more pleasant things. I will show you round the cave complex, and you will gain a better appreciation of how you will live."

The cave was pleasantly cool, and the prince stared agog at the amazing marble statues in niches around the walls of the cavern they were in. The Monitor interrupted the prince's musings and pointed out the key features of the living area inside the huge cavern. There were some five beds cum couches for resting and sleeping spread equally round the periphery of the living area. Round the lovely curved table in the center of the living area, there were six beautifully handmade chairs.

Four large storage cupboards were strategically located round the cavern. Bowls containing fruit and vases of flowers were positioned on some of the open storage cupboards' shelves. The prince noted that some of the flowers were wilting and needed to be replaced.

"I have a love of nature, and the flowers maintain my good spirits. We will collect some fresh ones from the mountainside to replace the wilted ones when you are ready. We will, however, now complete our tour of the cave complex," said the Monitor.

The prince was then led into a small offshoot of the cavern, which contained a woodstove and oven. "We do all our cooking in here,' said the Monitor. "We make bread, roast our meat, and cook the vegetables. It will be your job to collect the wood for the stove and oven with my assistance as required. The glazed earthenware mugs always hang up on the rack over there, so make sure that is where they are placed after use and when they have been washed. You will have noted that we keep the various metal plates, pans, and other cooking utensils on the shelving over there."

He then led the prince through the wooden gate into the stable area. Ajax and the prince's horse were munching contentedly on the hay from a stone bier. Close-by was another stone bier filled with water. The floor was covered with straw. "Your duties will be to clean out the stable on a daily basis and lay fresh straw. It is also required, after you have accomplished that, you ensure the horses' bier is filled with fresh hay and the other bier is filled with fresh water. The straw and horse droppings that you remove from the stable along with the vegetable wastage is placed in a natural alcove behind the cave. This forms good compost for the plants and bushes and fruit trees. We regularly turn over the compost to facilitate an even texture.

"A further duty is to periodically take the carpets outside the cavern on a systematic basis and beat the accumulated dust out of them. You will also be responsible for obtaining fresh milk from the goats and making butter and cheese from their milk. There are also other duties that will arise from time to time, but there will be nothing that you cannot handle.

"However, please be aware that you will be fully supported by me when undertaking your duties, and I am always at hand if you have any problems or wish to discuss anything. I will now show you the rest of the cave complex. However, before I do that, I will give you a gold disk to hang around your neck; it has the same functions as my own, and you must guard it very closely and never let it out of your sight. You will need the disk to move in and out of the cavern complex and to communicate with me when required. I will explain the various functions of the disk as needed, so do not be concerned about it."

The Monitor next led the prince into the main storeroom off the central cavern which contained sacks of flour, yeast extract, olives, figs and other fruits, as well as a range of herbs and vegetables. These were stored in urns, baskets, and vases as well as sacks made of a coarse but very strong material.

A farther storeroom led off the central cavern, and this contained the bales of straw for spreading on the stable floor. It also held a rich supply of hay for the horses' feed.

Subsequent to seeing the last storeroom, the Monitor walked to a spring in the corner of the cavern from which bubbled out cool, crystal clear, and fresh mountain water. He explained that the water continually circulated round and was filtered through a gravel bed and, hence was always fresh. It was very pleasant for human consumption as well as to give to the horses and was to be used for the Monitor and the prince to bathe and wash in.

The Monitor then said, "The next thing we need to discuss is your training and development. This will be quite comprehensive and cover such things as spiritual healing and development, reading and writing skills, mathematics and science, problem solving concepts, and verbal and nonverbal communication. There will be other subject matter, concepts, and applications as you are ready to assimilate them. You will note that your training consists of theoretical concepts and the associated practical applications. You will also learn and gain experience of technology far beyond the imagination and experience of any one on this planet. So having given you an insight into the various facets of your training and development as well as your duties around the cavern complex, do you have any questions?"

"No doubt with your assistance, master, it will not take too long for me to become accustomed to my duties round the cavern complex. I have also been subject to some personal learning through a wise tutor; but from what you have told me, I think it was not as comprehensive as the training I will receive from you. I am very excited about the knowledge I will acquire and am sure it will be of considerable benefit to me," responded the prince. He pointed to a door, barely discernible as it formed part of the cave wall. "What is through there, master?'

The Monitor replied, "Through that door is the secret of the technology I referred to, which if applied judiciously, will ensure that as emperor, you will lead Atlantis to a glorious future. However, as yet you are not ready to experience it; so be patient, young prince, and all will subsequently be revealed."

CHAPTER 6

Taming of the Wild Creatures and the Village Encounter

It was amazing how quickly the time passed by, and in no time at all, the prince was ready to celebrate his eighteenth birthday. During his time with the Monitor he had applied himself diligently to his studies and worked hard at completing his various duties. Delighted at the progress achieved by the prince, the Monitor made a special effort to ensure he was effectively tutored in all aspects of the specified subject matter. The theoretical teaching was regularly reinforced by practical, hands-on experience round and outside the cave facilities in the Charis mountains and nearby forest.

The prince exercised every day, and in conjunction with this, he enjoyed good food and led an active outdoor life. He also undertook the hard work demanded by his duties round the cavern and surrounding mountainside. This resulted in him filling out and growing tall, strong, and muscular.

He learned about the herbs and edible fruit and vegetables growing in both the garden and the forest. This resulted in his becoming an excellent cook and skilled at the preparation of the various medications. The acquired skills in spiritual healing and development and learning gained in providing direct assistance to the Monitor, in treating the villagers resulted in his rapidly gaining a reputation as a skilled healer in his own right.

The grateful villagers were quite willing to provide the flour, yeast extract, and other required provisions in return for the healing provided by the Monitor and his handsome apprentice. They also appreciated the rich fruit and prophylactic vegetables provided by the Monitor. The huge return from the garden and forest was a result of the considerable skill displayed by the prince in support of the Monitor.

On reflecting on the years spent with the Monitor, a couple of exacting experiences stood out for the prince and which were particularly memorable. First, he remembered when, at thirteen years of age, he was trained to communicate with the animals. This was initially with their two horses, and then when the prince had mastered this technique, he was taken into the forest for an even more challenging experience.

The Monitor and prince traveled into the forest until they came across a pack of wolves. The wolf pack leader, a huge white animal, glared at them; and the prince's knees knocked and his blood ran cold. Sensing the prince's fear, the Monitor said, "Have courage, boy; this is your opportunity to make a significant breakthrough in your training and development. Do not hesitate, walk boldly up to the pack leader, fill your heart with compassion for the animal, and apply the other skills you have acquired."

The prince took a deep breath, and summoning up all of his courage, he strode toward the pack leader. He almost turned tail and ran when the wolf snarled at him and stiffened its muscular frame as if it was about to attack. The huge animal had powerful jaws, which the prince realized could tear him apart. However, he hesitated only momentarily before pushing forward. He pressed the crystal in the center of the gold disk around his neck as hard as he could and focused all his attention on reaching the animal's mind. The wolf gave him a quizzical look and held its head to one side. It then trotted over to the prince and prowled in a concentric circle round him, occasionally moving in to brush against his legs. The prince stroked the wolf and whispered softly into its ear. He never once relinquished his grip on the red crystal during this time.

Eventually the wolf trotted off, leading the pack away from the Monitor and the prince. The Monitor was delighted with the outcome. "Well done, Euthymios; you have moved forward and achieved something special this day. Your mother would have been really proud of you, as indeed am I."

The next thing the prince recalled was when, at sixteen years of age, he was given the task of collecting the healing berries required by the Monitor from a cave high in the Charis mountains. The berries were black in color and the same size as small olives and of the same constituency. They hung down from thick vines in bunches, just like grapes, at the rear of the cave.

He rode his horse to a convenient spot, close to where he intended to climb up to the cave containing the vines of healing berries. He tethered his horse to a low tree branch and made sure he was fully prepared for the climb up the mountain.

Euthymios took a long, hard look up toward the cave; and after a few moments' hesitation, commenced his climb up the mountainside. He had an empty backpack for holding the bunches of healing berries. He also had a medical pack and specially designed machete fastened to a belt at his side. The machete was needed to cut the bunches of healing berries off the strong, tough vines. With considerable effort, the prince fought his way up the mountain until finally he was able to pull himself up and stand on a broad ledge situated outside the cave complex containing the vines of healing berries. When he had regained his composure, he entered the largest cave. He paused a little way inside the cave entrance and waited until his eyes adjusted to the dark condition. When his eyes became accustomed to the subdued light in the cave, he was alarmed to see a huge mountain lion at the rear of the cave, in front of the vines of healing berries. The prince knew that if he was to gather the required bunches of healing berries, let alone survive, he would have to communicate with the lion.

He cautiously approached the mountain lion and noticed it was favoring its right front paw. Once again the prince took a firm grip on the red crystal in the center of the gold disk, and he went into a state of deep concentration. The lion gazed quizzically at him and watched quietly as the prince then approached and gently took its paw into his hand. The prince then slowly released his grip on the crystal and firmly grasped the sharp piece of flint in the lion's paw and pulled it out in one fluid movement. He then took a leather container of ointment from his medical pack and gently rubbed it into the wounded paw. Noting that the lion was quite settled, the prince took a strip of bandage from the pouch and tied it in position. He then gently stroked the lion while he whispered in its ear. He knew that the bandage would last just long enough for the lion's wound to heal before it falls off.

Following this procedure, the prince backed away and waited until he was sure the lion was not going to make any threatening move toward him. Then summoning all of his courage, Euthymios boldly walked by the side of the animal and commenced to fill his backpack with bunches of the healing berries he cut from the thick vine. His well-made, razor-sharp machete cut like butter through the vine under the powerful strokes from his youthful yet strong muscular arms. Soon he had filled the backpack, and he then slowly backed away from the lion and out of the cave. He breathed a deep sigh of relief, ensured his back pack was secure, and commenced the long climb down the mountain. It was slow going, as the backpack was very heavy under the weight of the bunches of healing berries, but he gradually inched his way down.

Euthymios had selected a different way down the mountain, believing that this would make for an easier descent. However, when he had reached a wide ledge, he dropped off his backpack and leaned back against the cliff face, quite exhausted. Despite his exhaustion, he breathed a sigh of relief at having climbed down past the most difficult part of the mountain. His relief was cut short when, farther along the ledge on which he was resting, he noticed an eagle's nest full of young chicks. Stiffening his legs and back to reinforce his position against the mountain face, the prince looked anxiously round for the mother eagle. He did not have too long to wait before he saw it swooping down on him. The eagle dived down on him with a screaming cry, wildly flapping its wings, and the prince almost tumbled off the ledge as he took evasive action.

He realized that communicating with the eagle would be even more challenging than with the mountain lion. Despite this, he determined that to kill the eagle and leave the chicks to starve to death was not an option. Hence, he took a deep breath and as the eagle wheeled, ready to come in for the next attack, took a firm grip on the crystal and concentrated as never before. The eagle geared up for the next attack; and the prince, in deep concentration, was totally helpless should it swoop in at him. However, the eagle hesitated and then swooped in on the nest and settled next to the young eaglets. The prince released his grip on the crystal and resumed his descent and, at last, reached the bottom of the mountain without further incident.

The prince loaded the backpack, machete, and medical pack onto his horse and set off at a fast pace for the cave. When he arrived home, he related his adventures in the mountain to the Monitor.

The Monitor was delighted with the success of the prince's mission, and slapping him on the back, exclaimed, "Congratulations, I am really proud of you. You did extremely well to communicate with a wounded animal, and then you top that off with a mother eagle protecting its chicks. I admire your great courage; your training and development is going very well."

However, the prince's reminiscing was interrupted by the Monitor, which brought him back to the present. "Come on, Euthymios, we are going into the village to collect a few supplies. While we are there, we will collect something special for your birthday."

The prince soon had the horse and trap ready, and they set off for the village. It was not too long before they reached the outskirts of the village and heard the excited shouts and delighted screams of the children at the market.

They left the horse and trap at the livery stable and walked into the marketplace. The rich hues of the canopies as well as the well laid out stalls loaded with all sorts of clothing, household items, fruit and vegetables made for a very colorful environment. The prince was delighted that he and the Monitor were there.

They collected their supplies and loaded them onto the trap in the livery stable. When they had finished loading the supplies, they walked back to the market place.

Suddenly they heard a loud shouting and noticed two soldiers haranguing a stallholder. They were arguing over the cost of the swords they were trying to buy. Tired of the tirade of abuse, the stallholder shrugged his shoulders and put the swords away and turned to attend to another customer.

One of the soldiers grabbed the stallholder and dragged him to the ground and snarled, "Don't ignore me, you little runt, or I'll run you through. We are soldiers of the Emperor Lycus, and when we want something, we get it. So I think I'll just kill you anyway and we'll take the swords."

The prince ran up and shouted, "Leave him alone, you bullies; pick on someone your own size."

One of the soldiers turned on the prince, unsheathed his sword, and exclaimed, "Well, what have we here then; looks like some upstart that needs to be brought down to size. I think I'll start by cutting off his ears, and then we'll both have some fun with him."

The Monitor knew it was time for him to intercede, and he held up his hand and exclaimed, "You are very brave against an inexperienced youth, but unfortunately for you, I am here to put an end to your fun. However before I do that, I have a surprise for you if you dare to take up the challenge?"

"What challenge can you provide, old man? Show us what you have, and then we'll have our fun with you after we've taken care of the youth," sneered the soldier.

The Monitor took the gold chain from around his neck and held it so that he could rotate the circular disk on it and allow the large red crystal in the center to brightly flash. He said in a soft voice to the two soldiers, "Look deeply into the jewel, feel its power vibrating through your whole body, and soak up its strength." The fascinated soldiers gazed, totally absorbed at the crystal and were soon hypnotized.

The Monitor said to the soldiers, "Your behavior has shown that you are both swine, and as such, you will exhibit your reflected behavior. So get down on all fours and crawl around grunting and squealing and sniffing the ground until I tell you to stop." He allowed the soldiers to act out their role as swine for a long time. Meanwhile, a large crowd had gathered, and having all suffered under the brutality of the baron's soldiers, laughed and ridiculed them. The Monitor allowed this to go on for some time before he called a halt and brought the soldiers out of their trance. The soldiers then carried out the instructions the Monitor had given them, which was to forget all about their hypnotic experience, reimburse the stallholder for the insults he sustained, and to then rejoin their troop.

When the soldiers had gone, the Monitor approached the stallholder and said, "I would like to collect the special sword and scabbard you have made for me if they are ready?"

The stallholder collected the sword, which was in its scabbard, from the rear of the stall and handed it to the Monitor. An astounded Euthymios looked in awe at the exquisitely decorated scabbard and was full of wonder for the craftsman who had produced such admirable work. When the sword was withdrawn from the scabbard by the Monitor, it sparkled in the sun. It was made of special alloys and manufactured to the Monitor's precise specifications. The Monitor tested it out and then held it up with one finger and tried its balance. "It is a beautiful piece of work, Armallios, as is the scabbard; you have excelled yourself. Would you please let me know what I owe you for such fine pieces of work?"

The stallholder replied, "I have never enjoyed myself so much for a long time. It was a pleasure to see how the emperor's soldiers were made to look so foolish. I ask only that you provide personal healing to me and my family when we are ill. If you will promise to do this for me then the sword and scabbard are yours."

The Monitor responded, "That is but a small price to pay, and I accept. Should you or any of your family need me, seek me out at the foot of the Charis mountains, and I will race to your aid."

The Monitor then turned to Euthymios and said, "Here, these are your birthday presents," and handed him the sword and scabbard. "Look after them, and they will serve you well. We will have to make sure you can use such a beautiful weapon in a highly skilled manner."

A delighted Euthymios could hardly wait to strap the scabbard containing the sword around his waist. He then drew the sword and danced around, making a few practice thrusts and other movements.

"Enough, Euthymios, you will have plenty of time to practice your swordsmanship. Go and fetch the horse and trap, so we can be on our way," said the Monitor.

The Monitor then said his goodbye to the stallholder, after Euthymios returned with a refreshed and well-fed horse and the trap from the livery stables. The last time they had been to the village, they had traded Ajax and the prince's horse, plus some of the Monitor's gold, for one much younger. Hence when they set off to return to the cavern, it was at a lively pace.

Meanwhile, the two soldiers were sought out by one of the villagers, a greedy treacherous rogue. He, who was always on the lookout for a quick reward, informed them about what had happened; and the soldiers roared with uncontrollable rage.

"We'll take care of those ignorant villagers; they'll bitterly regret the day they ever laughed at our misfortune. Provide us with the names of those villagers who were watching when we were bewitched by this so-called healer, and you'll have your reward."

The informer gave the names of the villagers to the two soldiers and was handed a small bag of gold. When he had received his reward, he scurried away before the soldiers changed their mind.

"We'll take care of this healer and his apprentice, and then we'll go back to the village and retrieve our gold and obtain a lot more as compensation for our trouble," one of the soldiers said. "Now let us find our companions."

The two soldiers soon caught up with their five companions, and they related what had happened to them at the market.

"You were obviously bewitched by a powerful sorcerer, and we need to teach him and his apprentice a lesson they'll never forget. We'll make sure that they rue the day they ever took advantage of the emperor's soldiers. However, we'll need to mount up and chase after them straight away. They can't have traveled very far, and you said the villager informed you that they are headed for the foothills of the Charis mountains?" queried the troop leader.

"That's right," responded one of the soldiers who had been hypnotized. "I can't wait to catch up with them and watch them scream, as we have our way with them."

The soldiers collected their horses from the livery stable and set off at a fast gallop after the Monitor and the prince. Meanwhile, sensing that they might be in danger, the Monitor spurred his horse on to a greater effort. However, it was not too long before the prince, glancing round, spotted the seven riders. "We are being chased by the two soldiers and their five companions, master, and I do not think we can outrun them."

"Hold on, Euthymios," the Monitor said to the prince. "I'm going to make a run for that small mound over on the right hand side. That is where we will make our stand."

They reached the mound, and the Monitor jumped onto the back of the trap and placed his hand on the crystal, concentrated, and the front of the compartment flew open and a tray slid out. The Monitor lifted out of the tray what he called a photonic blaster, which fitted snugly round and conformed to the shape of his hand. He then jumped down from the trap, displaying surprising agility for his age, and took up position behind the mound.

By this time the emperor's soldiers were closing in rapidly on the Monitor's position. He took careful aim and discharged the photonic blaster at the nearest rider. A large hole appeared on the chest of the soldier's body armor, and he fell dead, backward and off his horse, with the impact. The Monitor systematically picked off each soldier until the last two were almost on top of him.

He just had time to fire wildly at one of the riders, and the soldier fell of his horse with half his head missing. The other soldier dived off his mount and over the mound, and his sword flew out of his hand. The soldier's shoulder crashed into the chest of the Monitor, and he went flying backwards with the force of the impact. He landed heavily on his back with the breath knocked completely out of his body. The soldier made a comparatively soft landing and was the first to recover his composure.

He grabbed the Monitor by the throat and said between gritted teeth, "Sorcerer, for what you have done to my comrades, I'm going to strangle the life out of you, and then I'm going to settle with your apprentice."

As the soldier's grip tightened round the Monitor's throat, he gradually lost consciousness and realized he was about to die. Sometime later, the Monitor regained consciousness and looked around to see the soldier lying face down on the ground with blood pouring from a deep wound on his back.

"I had to kill the soldier, master, otherwise you would surely have died," exclaimed Euthymios. "When he had his hands around your throat, I became desperate to save you. So I drew my sword, and grasping it in both hands, I plunged the blade into the unprotected part of his back with all of my strength. He gave a loud cry and released his grip on your throat, and I managed to pull his body off you. I have been waiting anxiously praying that you would make a full recovery."

"You have done well, Euthymios; and thanks to you, I am safe and well. I can see that you are ready to further your education, and we will discuss this when we reach home. However, we must first visit the gypsy camp close to here and consult with the head of the gypsies. You will no doubt recall that he is both a friend and a customer of ours?"

"Yes, I remember him; you went to his aid when a contagious disease broke out, in his camp,' replied Euthymios. The Monitor nodded, picked up the photonic blaster which was lying nearby and climbed back into the trap. He again grasped the crystal and concentrated to open the hidden compartment and replace the blaster. When the Monitor climbed down from the trap, the curious Euthymios inquired, "What is that strange weapon, master; it is like nothing I have seen before?"

The Monitor responded, "Do not concern yourself about that, Euthymios; soon all will be revealed, just be patient."

They mounted the trap and set off for the gypsy camp, arriving after a short drive. The Monitor was warmly greeted by the gypsies in the camp. The head of the gypsies stepped forward with a broad grin on his face and with his arms outstretched, and he and the Monitor embraced. "What can I do for you my friend; it is not long since you were last here?" queried the gypsy.

"We have had a run in with some of the emperor's soldiers. Seven of them are lying dead, a short ride from here to the south. If you go straight away, you can keep their armor, weapons, horses, gold, and whatever else you find. I only ask that you bury the dead soldiers so they will never be found after you have stripped their bodies of everything of value. I want you to make certain that their deaths can never be traced back to me or Euthymios."

"My old friend, I hate the emperor and his soldiers like poison. They constantly harass us, demand money and goods, and rape our women and physically abuse us. It will be a pleasure to take their possessions and bury their corpses, and do not worry, their bodies will never be found. Incidentally, I do not want to know how you and your apprentice killed seven hardened warriors; it is enough that they are dead," said the gypsy with a chuckle. "Stay until I return, and we will talk some more and celebrate the death of the soldiers. Incidentally, the weapons and armor will never be traced after the villager named Armallios has worked on them; he is a skilled artisan when working with metals."

"I am well aware of the skills of Armallios; he has done some good work for me over the years," responded the Monitor. 'However, much as I would love to stay, my apprentice and I must be home before dark. May the gods go with you, and I will take my leave. Until we meet again, my friend."

The Monitor and Euthymios then resumed their journey, and the gypsies rode off to collect their booty. On arriving back at the cavern complex, the Monitor and Euthymios unloaded their supplies, and then the prince uncoupled the horse from the trap and ensured it was fed and watered and rubbed down. Euthymios prepared a meal, and after they had eaten, he and the Monitor went to rest for the night.

CHAPTER 7

Primitive Times and Adventures on the Monitor's Planet

Next morning, the Monitor awoke and dressed, had breakfast, and then looked around for Euthymios. Hearing shouts outside the cave, he cautiously made his way to the entrance. He looked out and saw Euthymios dancing around flashing the sword and making a series of cuts, thrusts, and parries. He had a fierce, determined look on his face as he practiced with the weapon.

"Well done, Euthymios, you cut a fine figure; how many of our enemies have you killed?" inquired the Monitor.

Euthymios lowered the sword and looked sheepishly at the Monitor. "It is a fine weapon, master; I cannot thank you enough for such a beautiful present."

"You can thank me, Euthymios, by practicing until you and the sword are as one. However, I consider it is now time to move into the next phase of your development. Today, I will expose you to a key technology that I rescued from the shuttlecraft when I and my companions traveled to this world from our home planet. You will be subject to what we call the dilatation procedure to enhance your strength and intelligence. This will not only ensure you are the finest warrior in Atlantis, but as your intelligence develops, you will be able to fully appreciate the complexity and scope of the technology salvaged from the spacecraft that was used to land me on this world."

"Is the dilatation procedure painful, master? Does it require any special skills?' inquired Euthymios.

The Monitor laughed. "No, Euthymios, it is not in the least painful; and you have all the qualifications to gain the maximum benefit from the procedure. You enter a cabinet in the technology room and stand on the circular plate in the center. I will program the computer and start the machine. You should just relax and feel the waves of energy flow all over and through you. The process will then rigorously examine every aspect of your intelligence and physique before subjecting you to the developmental procedure.

"You will know that the process is completed when the energy waves no longer course through your body. Then when the process is finished, you will be physically stronger and like lightening in your reflexes and movements. Your thinking will be enhanced so you can undertake the most complex of tasks and anticipate every move of any of the opponents you will face in combat or mental and physical challenge."

"Have you been through this procedure, master?" inquired Euthymios.

"Many years ago; far more than I care to remember. Now I am well and truly past my best and in the twilight of my long life. The demands made on my mind and body to enable me to last through to this century have taken a heavy toll," responded the Monitor. "Anyway, come into the room containing the respective equipment, Euthymios. Remember that you are required to enter the dilatation chamber naked."

Euthymios shed his clothes and entered the chamber, which consisted of a square cabinet with transparent sides and a solid opaque top. Once he was inside the chamber, the door was locked into place. The Monitor went to a nearby control panel and pulled down a control lever, and the screen on the panel lit up. The Monitor set the various controls on the panel, and a blue light lit up the interior of the chamber. After a short time, statistical information appeared on the screen, and the Monitor adjusted the panel controls until he was satisfied that the required statistical information had appeared. This information catered for the intelligence level and physical attributes of the person in the chamber. If this was not done before the dilatation process commenced, the individual in the chamber could sustain severe physical and/or brain damage.

The Monitor then set the dilatation process in motion via the control panel. There was a low hum from the machine during the prolonged dilatation process before the procedure was finally completed. Once the process was finished, the door slid open and Euthymios fell out of the dilatation chamber into the arms of the Monitor. Euthymios staggered along as though drunk and made it difficult for the Monitor to hold him up. They finally reached Euthymios's bed, and he collapsed onto it and fell into a deep sleep.

Euthymios slept for two days before he finally woke from his deep slumber. He threw off the blanket, arose, dressed, and had something to eat. When he had finished eating, he walked out of the cave and saw the Monitor in thoughtful contemplation. "What are you thinking about, master?" queried Euthymios.

"Your going through the dilatation process caused me to think quite deeply about the events leading up to my arrival on this world and what has occurred since I landed here. It really has been an incredible adventure. Come sit down and make yourself comfortable, and I will tell you the whole story. Despite the stimulation of your intelligence, you will find it is difficult to comprehend a lot of what I am saying. However, do not concern yourself as in the long run, the relevant aspects of what I am saying will be understood to provide the knowledge you require in your battle to regain the throne of Atlantis.

"You will recall that I said that I am not from this world. However, my home planet is very much like this one, only slightly larger. It is situated in another galaxy, and your world was only reached when the starship in which I was traveling plunged through a wormhole in the space-time continuum. These wormholes are randomly spaced and tend to move around rather than remain in a fixed position. I will explain our wormhole adventure later on in my discussion.

"We began as a species of animal life, as in the case of the human race, one amongst many others. Like humans, our race were more aggressive than most of the other we encountered. However, while you are descended from mammals, our species are descended from dinosaurs. I will explain more about this later in my narrative and the role we played in the destruction of the dinosaurs on your world. However, we certainly did not intend to destroy dinosaur life on the Earth, and it is something for which I am still deeply distressed.

"Our world has an atmosphere akin to that of Earth except that it is richer in oxygen. The consequence of this is that life on our planet tends to be significantly larger than that on this world. We have huge insects, and it is a constant battle to hold them at bay. In fact, if our species had originated from Earth, then we would probably have been a lot shorter than humans rather than being approximately the same size. Our planet is also somewhat drier than this world although we still have oceans and seas and plenty of fresh waters in our rivers.

"So you can gather from what I am saying that my people are descended from a relatively small, carnivorous breed of dinosaur. They had no scruples in their dealings with the other animal life and ruthlessly annihilated other species that they considered a threat. My ancestors left records of their mass genocide of other species in the form of drawings on the walls of the caves in which they lived.

"In many ways, we have a lot in common with the human race. We deliver our young live, and they are suckled by the females of our race, and we are warm blooded. We look after our young and guide them until they are the equivalent of five human years of age. They are then sent to training and development centers, and we occasionally visit them and obtain feedback on their progress. They come home to us during the holiday breaks, and we can volunteer to serve as helpers in the centers if we are willing or required.

"While we are approximately the same height and build as humans, we are decidedly lizardlike in appearance, and our faces and bodies are covered in red scales. We have two arms and two legs the same as you except that we have a short tail, which in our later development shrank and almost disappeared as it was of no practical value. We also have a thumb and four fingers, which developed from our dinosaur talons, hence the reason they are narrower and more pointed than yours."

"If that was your physical appearance on your home world, master, how is it that you look as human as the rest of the people here?" inquired Euthymios.

"That is a good point, Euthymios; well, the dilatation unit is a very versatile machine. As well as accomplishing the changes to you, Euthymios, I found that it could also change the physical appearance of members of our race. The process from our kind to yours is very complex and involves a number of sessions in the dilatation machine," responded the Monitor.

"It truly is a wonderful machine; who invented it?" inquired Euthymios.

"It was developed by a race of ancient beings that are not of either of our worlds and technologically are much more advanced. I will explain how I came into possession of the dilatation machine later in my narrative. Is there anything else you wish to ask me at this juncture?" inquired the Monitor.

"I have many questions, but I am sure you will answer them when the time is right. However, I find it difficult to believe that such a compassionate person as yourself could be descended from a murderous and barbaric species. Surely, your direct ancestors were a more peace-loving people?" replied Euthymios.

"Thank you for your comments, but what happened in the past needs to be accepted, and then we must move on. However, perhaps an example will illustrate how barbaric our ancestors could be. There are a number of drawings on cave walls that clearly illustrate the terrible massacres undertaken by our people. The story of this was related to me by my father.

"My distant ancestors lived in a fertile valley covered in lush grass which was, like on other areas of Galenos, a much darker green than on Earth. We have purple, red, and brown trees with long multi-colored strands and a lot with broad palmlike leaves and also multi-covered bushes with jagged leaves and some with sharp spikes. The blossoms on the bushes and other plants are breathtaking and truly exotic, consisting of a variety of shapes and sizes with brilliant colors. Unfortunately, there are species of our plant life which are quite poisonous although a lot produces a plethora of different edible fruit. The plant life on our world has also learned to adapt to a significantly drier atmosphere than that on Earth.

Our people had to be constantly on guard against attack by the diversity of insect life in the valley, some of them particularly poisonous. They lost a number of the tribe from insect attack but managed to keep this to a minimum.

This was facilitated by the traps they set and secretions from plant life that was discovered that either discouraged the insects or killed them when ingested.

"However, there was one insect species that was particularly difficult to control, and that was a large black species of ant. They were particularly aggressive and attacked anything whether or not it was regarded as prey. They delivered their intensely painful sting by gripping their prey with their powerful jaws (mandibles) and curling up their abdomen to expose the sting, which they used to inject the poison. Each ant was as large as a rat on Earth and had a bright red head and abdomen. They were highly poisonous; however, the poison was slow to act and anyone bitten would die in agony. Once the victim was dying from the ant bites, the ants would swarm all over the body and strip it bare.

"The ants built an extensive network of underground tunnels with chambers for the queen's residence, food storage, ant eggs, and the recently hatched young and for other functions. It was normally ensured that the entrance to the nest was well hidden in case of incursion by predators. They would stay at the one location until the food source was exhausted; the colony, led by the queen, would then move on until another more appropriate location was found.

"One day, in the search for another location, the ants invaded our tribe's valley while our tribal members were out hunting and gathering fruit and edible plants. Before they were aware of what was happening, three of the woman gathering plants and fruit close to where the ants had decided to make their incursion into the valley were surrounded.

"They had their backs to the river that flowed through the valley, and this was the only way of escape. However, the river was infested with a predatory species of large fish that had strong, razor sharp teeth. The fish were a major source of food for the tribe although their flesh was somewhat tough, when slowly cooked with the herbs the tribe gathered in the valley, it was quite edible.

"One of the women was so terrified of the ants, she jumped straight into the water and started to swim to the other side. She managed to make her way halfway across the river before she was savagely attacked by the fish. This caused her to scream out with the agonizing pain, and shout for help, and throw up her arms in agony. The water boiled and foamed and was soon dyed a dark red with the woman's blood. The woman sank to the bottom of the river while the fish tore huge strips of flesh from her body. It was not long before her body was stripped to the bone.

"The other two women could only look on in horror and stand in paralyzed shock, gazing at where their friend had entered the river. Distracted by the death of their friend, they were totally unprepared for the attack by the ants that swarmed all over them. The ants then systematically cut away the flesh from their bodies while the two women, still alive, screamed in agonized pain. They were soon on the ground, rolling from side to side in an endeavor to shake off the ants. However, it was all in vain, and the ants intensified their attack on the women. Mercifully, death finally came to the two women, and the ants continued the feeding process until there was only a pile of bones left on the ground.

"The rest of the tribe had retreated to the other side of the river and watched in absolute horror the fate of the women. They asked the tribal chief what they should do, and he realized that they had to take immediate action. He, therefore, ordered twenty of the tribe's warriors, some twelve men and eight women, to work their way behind the ants and set fire to the grass. The grass was tinder dry and knee high and would burn fiercely when set alight. The wind was fortunately blowing toward the river, which meant that the ants' only escape would be across the river containing the predatory fish.

"The warriors ran as quickly as they could and gradually worked their way behind the ant colony and lit the torches they carried. They then systematically set fire to the grass and watched the flames leap high into the air. Unfortunately, four of the warriors had moved in too close to the ant column and, while lighting the grass, were overwhelmed by a group of the ants. The rest of the warriors were powerless to assist their colleagues and could only move as fast as they could, away from the ant army. Once in a safe position, they stood in in silent horror, listening to the anguished cries of their colleagues.

"Meanwhile, the fire took a firm hold and raced through the ranks of the ants. The insects let out a weird, high-pitched scream as the fire overwhelmed them. Loud crackling sounds could be heard as the fire burned through each ant's body. To escape the fierce heat, the leading ants raced into the river followed by their colleagues. The river boiled following the rush of ants into the water, and a sudden savage attack on the insects by the predatory fish. The ants tried unsuccessfully to defend themselves, but they were at a severe disadvantage in the water. When not drowned, the insects were killed by the huge bites taken out of their bodies by the carnivorous fish. A strong undercurrent continually carried the dead insects down the river so there was never a buildup of carcasses. Eventually, all of the ants that had entered the river were dead and their bodies carried away.

"There were only a small number of ants that had escaped the fire, and they were ruthlessly hunted down by the tribe's warriors. Finding that they were leaderless, they tended to wander aimlessly around, completely disorientated, and were speared, clubbed, or killed by arrow by the incensed warriors. Unfortunately, the warriors attacked by the ants as they lit the fires had died an agonizing death.

"We shared the valley with another tribe from a different dinosaur root; they were slightly bigger than our people and had dark blue scales. They were essentially a peace-loving people but could fiercely defend their territory if required. We shared an uneasy peace with that tribe, but unfortunately, the tension between us was exacerbated by the fact that we had not consulted them about the ants. They were incensed that that the grass had been set alight and claimed that if the wind had changed, it could easily have raged out of control and destroyed their homes and food-gathering areas. The fact that the whole of their tribe could have been burned to death absolutely infuriated them.

"The situation totally deteriorated when one day, Herodius, one of the young men of our tribe, breathlessly raced in from the forest. 'Murder!' he cried. 'A group of hunters from the neighboring tribe have killed Allidoram. One of the hunters strangled her when she would not let him have her way with her, and they then threw her over the cliffs onto the rocks below.'

"This incensed our tribe as they had already been involved in several fiery debates over the neighboring tribe's threat to take action over our tribe's encroachment on their hunting and food-gathering territory following the destruction of the black ants. So there was a general call to arms, and in the early dawn, an attack was launched against our neighbors. Although the neighboring tribesmen were caught unawares, they quickly rallied, and the fighting became exceptionally fierce. However, with the element of surprise, our tribe quickly gained the upper hand and subdued the opposing tribe's warriors. Unfortunately, with the blood lust burning fiercely in their bosoms, my ancestors were uncontrollable and went on a savage rampage. They slaughtered everyone in sight, men, women, and children until the area was ankle-deep in blood and every one of our neighbors was dead. It truly was a horrific sight as our warriors had huge machetes and hacked anyone who confronted them to pieces.

"When the fighting was over, our tribesmen made their way back to their camp. The atmosphere was very subdued as I think our people were actually ashamed of the slaughter. When they arrived back at the encampment, they were met by the tribe's witch doctor. He had been gathering herbs, bark, and other items for his medicines in the forest for the last week and had missed the feedback on the murder of Allidoram and the subsequent fighting.

"When everything had been explained to him, the witch doctor cried out, 'But it was Herodius who strangled Allidoram and then threw her body over the cliff. He did this because it was apparent that Allidoram wanted nothing to do with him. I was hidden from their view but could still witness everything that happened. It is a shame that I am aging and no longer able to keep up with the young warriors, otherwise, I may have been able to intervene. However, there is nothing wrong with my eyes.'

"When he heard this, the leader of our people went into a towering rage, realizing that the mass slaughter need never have happened. Despite the fact that Herodius was his own son, he seized a machete and chopped him to pieces.

"The unfortunate effect of the slaughter was that the blood and body parts, from the slain of the enemy tribe, attracted a range of predators, some of them extremely vicious. Hence, it was no surprise when a team of three hunters was ambushed by a particularly aggressive group of dinosaurs. The attack was cunningly staged by the dinosaurs; they surrounded the hunters and attacked from all sides. Hopelessly trapped, the hunters had no way of escape and were quickly overcome and torn to pieces and devoured.

"The leader of the tribe coordinated a tribal council meeting, following the attack on the three hunters. It was decided that the only thing to do was to move to another valley. So the tribe gathered their belongings together and set off for the nearest appropriate fertile region. On their journey, the tribe members were continually harassed and, when gathering food and water, attacked by the carnivorous dinosaurs; and at times, the carnage was horrifying. They eventually reached their destination with some forty percent of the tribe dead. Fortunately, the valley was uninhabited, and they were able to make a stand and fight off the pursuing predators.

"The valley was truly beautiful and even more pleasing to the eye than the tribe's last location. It was surrounded by hills containing numerous caves; hence, it had tremendous potential to become the perfect new home for the tribe. It was rich in fruit-bearing plants and contained a diverse amount of game, easily enough to satisfy the tribe's meat requirements. The river flowing through the center of the valley was fresh flowing and contained numerous edible fish. Whether fortunate or not, there was none of the carnivorous fish that infested the river in their previous home.

"However, they could not rest securely; as one day, one of the particularly vicious and cunning breed of dinosaurs managed to infiltrate the valley. The dinosaurs were as large as stallions with huge, powerful jaws and moved with lightning speed. The tribe only became aware of their presence when a group of the womenfolk was gathering berries. They were suddenly surrounded by the whole pack of fierce predators. They dropped their baskets of berries and tried to run, but there was no escape, and they were quickly overtaken and torn to pieces. The screams of the women echoed across the whole of the valley.

"Upon hearing the screams, the tribal warriors, both men and women, grabbed their weapons and raced to the scene of the carnage. The fighting was fierce and lasted until most of the dinosaurs were killed and the rest had been driven off. However, more than half of the warriors perished in the battle while another quarter was severely wounded. The sharp talons and huge jaws of the dinosaurs resulted in gaping wounds where a warrior's flesh was torn away.

"A tribal meeting was conducted after the battle and a new leader appointed to take the place of the one killed by the dinosaurs. It was decided to construct a high, solid wooden fence at the valley access points at either end of the valley. This was designed to stretch from the hills on the north side to those on the south side of the valley. It was meant to not only keep the savage dinosaurs at bay but also assist repel any invading tribesmen from outside the valley.

"The fence was constructed after many months of hard labor by the severely depleted tribe. It took its toll in additional lives, as during the course of the fence building, they had to fight off many marauding carnivores. One day, a large carnivorous dinosaur with huge jaws and long, razor sharp teeth attacked the tribesmen as they worked on constructing the fence. The dinosaur was heavily camouflaged with light and dark stripes to blend in with the surrounding trees and plants and, hence despite its size, was difficult to see. It crept up on the workers until quite close then it rushed them giving out a fearful roar. The workers ran for their lives but unfortunately a couple of them were stranded on top of the partially built fence. Despite the two workers' desperate and rapid descent the dinosaur was upon them before they reached the ground and seized the nearest worker in its mighty jaws. He screamed in agony as the monster's teeth sank into his body. The blood gushed out of the dinosaur's mouth and covered the other worker who stood, as though petrified, too frightened to move.

"He was suddenly aware of the danger he was in and raced away and joined his colleagues. They realized that they would have to take action, to destroy the dinosaur before it reached the rest of the tribe. It was however apparent that they did not have the means to kill the carnivore by direct attack so they decided on another strategy. They determined to lure the dinosaur to the top of the cliff, overlooking the river that flowed through the valley and somehow ensure it went over the cliff edge.

"Two of the quickest members of the group went back to where the dinosaur was still feasting on their colleague. It was apparent that the carnivore had almost completely devoured their colleague and was almost ready to move onto the next victim. Noting this, the tribesmen used their sling shots to aggravate the dinosaur and make it follow them. The dinosaur roared with anger and lumbered after the two tribesmen. They led the dinosaur to the cliff edge and started to run away. Unfortunately, the dinosaur stopped and turned to chase after them. Realizing what was happening, one of the men turned and ran back to the cliff edge and used his sling shot to pepper the carnivore with stones. The dinosaur roared with anger and charged toward the tribesman. He waited until the last minute and dived to one side. However, the weight of the dinosaur caused the whole of that part of the unstable cliff edge to collapse and both tribesman and carnivore fell into the river.

"The tribe searched the river and its banks, but there was no sign of their colleague. They finally realized he was gone and, while mourning his loss, gave thanks to their gods for the bravery of the missing tribesman. Undoubtedly if the dinosaur had not been stopped, it would have created carnage in the valley and led its colleagues back to the tribe.

"There were also a lot of accidental deaths from the heavy lifting and general construction work. So in retrospect, it can be appreciated what a magnificent job our tribesmen did in building those walls. The conditions were not only very dangerous and the construction work extremely difficult but they had only primitive tools and methods of lifting available to them."

CHAPTER 8

Global Warming and Economic Woes

"So the centuries went by, and our species became increasingly industrialized as they took the maximum advantage of technological change and other developments. Our world population increased dramatically due to the improved lifestyles facilitated by these developments. However, we still had a world consisting of individual self-governing countries, and this exacerbated any global issues requiring international agreement. These issues included the probability of mass starvation across the globe due to the rapidly increasing world population, which at the time of my birth, had reached eight billion people.

"Global warming was also something we totally ignored, as we recklessly allowed every kind of pollutant to be absorbed into the atmosphere. We also stood by and watched as the pollution increased due to the rapid growth of our industries and the heavily polluting fuel used for our powered vehicles and machines. The thing we never took into consideration was that energy is constantly flowing into the atmosphere in the form of sunlight from our hot, bright sun. While some of this sunlight is reflected back into space the rest is absorbed by the planet. Unfortunately, an unbalance occurred between the energy from the sun and that from the planet as a result of the polluting of our world. This caused dramatic changes to our climate, and a hazardous warming up of the environment.

"There were a number of serious repercussions as a result of this global warming. A catastrophic effect was that significant amounts of our formerly fertile land became much drier. This was not only due to an alarming decrease in rainfall but also because of our massive program of deforestation. The result was a dramatic encroachment on what was formerly fertile land by the desert. This had serious repercussions not only for our species but for our farm animals and the wildlife on the planet. There was an alarming loss of wildlife and a major number of species became extinct as their habitat disappeared and there were dramatic changes in the weather patterns.

"One of my uncles was commissioned to travel into the desert as part of an investigation to assess the damage to the countryside caused by global warming. He did this in his environmental officer role with the national government of our country. He traveled to the desert in his small armored transport vehicle with his trainee, both of them dressed in their area work clothes. The population of our planet wore clothes conducive to a climate, which was generally warmer than that on Earth. Our clothes were lightweight, relatively short, and generally consisted of just two separate garment pieces over our underclothes. Our clothing, like our bedding and other cloth items, was woven from the dense array of plants growing on our riverbanks.

"While they admired the beautiful desert scenery, they were shocked by the huge area of desert encroachment on what was formerly fertile land. The once beautiful trees and shrubs and rich deep grass had disappeared and was replaced by sparse areas of short desert scrub and the occasional cactus and groups of succulent plants.

"Everything went well with my uncle and his trainee's work until late in the second day of their investigation. They were examining a particular part of the desert area consisting of a deep ravine. The ravine normally had a wide river flowing through it, but this was now little more than a stream. They bent down to examine the stream and to take samples of the river water. Suddenly, a huge crocodilelike creature came rushing round a bend in the ravine face. When it sighted the two technicians, it opened its massive jaws and gave out a fearsome roar. The creature rushed at the two men, endeavoring to swim down the shallow river; however, it was so huge that its feet touched the bottom so that it was half-running and half-swimming.

"Unfortunately, the two technicians' vehicle was on top of the ridge and definitely too far out of their reach before the crocodile would be upon them. My uncle had also left his photonic blaster in his vehicle, as he had not anticipated any danger. However, the trainee was quick to react; he grabbed a heavy log from the riverbank and charged at the creature. He commenced to strike the crocodile across the head, with the log, and with a great snarl, it turned on him. The creature gripped the log in its jaws and tossed it to one side. The trainee turned to run, but the crocodile was too quick for him and grabbed him in its fearsome jaws. The technician screamed in fear and agony as the creature's powerful jaws bit through his body. Mercifully, death rapidly followed before the crocodile started to eat him.

"Knowing there was nothing he could do for his companion, my uncle cautiously commenced to climb up the side of the ravine. The crocodile suddenly realized my uncle was escaping and dropped the body of the trainee and raced after him. My uncle desperately climbed faster as the crocodile snapped at his heels. He reached his vehicle and placed his palm on the door and it slid open. He dropped into the driver's seat, pulled down the short handle on the dashboard and the engine roared into life.

"Meantime, the crocodile threw itself onto the back of the vehicle and tried to bit its way through the top, which had a square section of clear, reinforced Perspex. My terrified uncle desperately tried to drive the vehicle forward to escape the crocodile's attack, but it clung on tenaciously, and its fearsome jaws savagely attacked the Perspex panel. The vehicle shook as it strained to move forward, but it would not budge with the weight of the huge creature on its back.

"It was only a matter of time before his vehicle was totally bogged and the crocodile broke into the vehicle and seized him. His photonic blaster was useless to him while he was locked in his vehicle; firing it inside the vehicle could cause a back flash, which could seriously injure my uncle. So he knew he had only one option and decided to take it. The vehicle had a forward engine which was used for normal driving and a rear engine that was only scheduled to be used when the vehicle was bogged and could not be moved using normal power. When gunned, the rear engine would roar into life and burn a huge amount of his fuel in one enormous flame out.

"My uncle took a deep breath and gunned the rear engine. The escaping exhaust gases were very powerful, and as my uncle anticipated, they blasted the crocodile so powerfully that it released its hold on his vehicle and dropped, badly wounded, onto the ground. The creature rolled back and forth in anguish in its death throes.

"My uncle cut the vehicle engine, collected his photonic blaster from the compartment in his vehicle, and cautiously made his way up to the creature and, from a humane perspective, went to finished it off. However, when it saw my uncle emerge from his vehicle, the crocodile somehow, in its final moments of life managed to raise itself up on its legs and give out one last mighty roar. This caused my uncle to drop back in fright. However, the creature flopped back down and its death throes continued. My uncle then cautiously moved closer to the crocodile and shot it dead.

"He settled back into his vehicle, checked the reserve fuel tank, and was relieved to find it was almost full to capacity. The reserve tank was then switched on, the engine started, and my uncle cautiously drove, with every possible vehicle component turned off, to the nearest town, relieved to find he had made it out of the desert in one piece.

"My father's best friend, Gennordis, was a salesperson who traveled all over the various country areas, selling his company's farm equipment. As part of his next sales program, he settled into an area where he was confident he could make a considerable impact in the local market. He made his headquarters in the inn situated in the largest town in the area. This just happened to be situated on the coastal strip, and the view from the town promenade was truly magnificent. There was a beautiful beach leading off the promenade consisting of a huge stretch of golden sand. The sea lapped gently onto the beach and was a beautiful aquamarine color with gentle cream-colored breakers; it truly was a glorious sight.

"Gennordis made a great success of his sales program across the area and settled into the town and sent for his wife and family. They had a teenage son and girl a couple of years younger than the boy. They found a nice house, close to the promenade, and life was idyllic, that is, until one day there was a government warning of a massive tidal wave heading for the town. The huge tidal wave heading the family's way could have been caused by a number of things, i.e., earthquakes, landslides, volcanic eruptions, explosions, or meteorites. In this case, the cause was an underwater earthquake. Although there had been massive tidal waves occurring since the recorded history of our world, they had of late been occurring with increasing frequency and ferocity, coinciding with the advent of global warming. Indeed since global warming, we found we generally had a much greater frequency of violent storms and serious flooding across the whole planet.

"Gennordis gathered his family together and, after an indepth discussion, decided the safest option was to head for the water tower, which was a reasonable drive away. However, it was not long before a fierce storm struck the area, and the rain came on in a continuous downpour. Despite this, they pushed ahead and packed bags containing a supply of food and drink and took pillows and blankets and a change of clothing as well as toiletries.

"They reached the water tower; and fortunately, Gennordis, his wife and son and daughter were in great physical condition. Hence, the climb up the ladder on the exterior of the tower, while very demanding and slippery because of the continuous rain, did not deter the family members; and they eventually reached the top. It was amazing how many people were already there, so it took a while to find a reasonably dry spot in which they could settle. Gennordis and his son climbed back down the tower and, despite the continuous rain, were able to assemble a rope-and-pulley configuration. This was securely fastened on top of the tower by the remaining family members, and they were able to haul up all of their possessions. Once their vehicle had been unloaded, Gennordis and his son climbed back up to the top of the tower as quickly as possible.

"They did not have to wait long for the tidal wave to arrive, and it came with a thunderous roar. It rushed up the beach and through the town in one mountainous wall of water, carrying everything before it. Everyone held their breath as the water tower shook violently and rocked on its foundations; fortunately, the strongly built tower held firm as the water roared around it.

"Eventually the water subsided and withdrew until there were areas of the shoreline that had never been uncovered before. The damage across the town was horrific with buildings completely flattened; the wreckage of boats was washed up on the streets, and debris from the houses and surrounding park areas was strewn everywhere. Gennordis's vehicle was completely destroyed as were the vehicles of the other people on top of the tower. The dead bodies of numerous townspeople littered the streets, and the moans of the badly wounded could be heard clear across the town. It was pitiful and almost broke the hearts of those people on top of the tower.

"However, the family were relieved that they had survived the effects of the massive tidal wave and looked around to see if everyone else on the tower was safe. Everywhere there were people pointing and talking incessantly, and they all were relieved that they and their families were alive and well. Gennordis's son was particularly excited and leaned over the side of the tower to gain a better view of the damage at ground level. Unfortunately, a sudden gust of wind lifted his cap off his head, and it sailed down to the bottom of the tower.

"Gennordis's son rushed to the tower's ladder and started to climb down, and although his father was fast on his feet, he was unable to stop him. In vain, he yelled at his son to come back up to the top of the tower. So while he anxiously looked on, Gennordis's son completed his climb down the ladder and raced over and picked up his cap. He held it up in triumph to his father but looked around in alarm when his father pointed out to sea.

"The tide was on the turn, and a tidal wave more ferocious than before was roaring in toward them. Gennordis's son hesitated for only a few seconds and tucked his cap in his pocket and raced for the tower ladder. He clambered up the ladder as fast as he could while the unstoppable tidal wave raced toward him with incredible force. He gradually neared the top of the ladder as the tidal wave raced round the tower and hungrily reached up for him.

"Gennordis raced down the ladder and grabbed the collar of his son's jacket as the powerful tidal wave endeavored to tear him off the ladder. The boy cried out in fear as the water sucked at his body, and he lost his grip on the ladder. His father grimly hung onto his son, and just when he thought he was going to lose him, the water suddenly receded

"A feeling of relief rushed through Gennordis after he had pulled his son to safety. However, he still felt compelled to chastise his son for his foolhardiness. His son apologized for his behavior but informed his father that he could not stand to lose his lucky cap. His father was too relieved to take the matter any further and was just overjoyed to have his son escape the massive tidal wave. They hugged each other in relief and danced around in joy at their escape from the fierce floods.

"The town was totally devastated by the huge tidal wave, but Gennordis and his family were determined to stay and carve out a good life for themselves. So the whole family threw themselves into helping the town with the restoration initiatives, and with government assistance it came back to life. They were destined to spend many more years together in that area, enjoying the fruits of their labors.

"One of my father's cousins, Hepmarkas and his family, tired of the overcrowded and hectic lifestyle of the city decided to go somewhere where peace and tranquility prevailed. Hepmarkas was a computer program designer and was employed on a contract basis and worked from home. Hence his plans for a move away from the city was not going to adversely affect his work. His wife was also a trained school teacher, and so she and her husband resolved to provide home tutoring for the children. So they relocated to a sparse area on the edge of the South Pole, building a house to meet their specific needs. Their life was solitary but stimulating, and once they became used to the bitter cold winters and brief summers, very enjoyable. However as the years raced by, they noticed a decided warmth in the climate. There was a measurable retreat of the glaciers and melting of the ice cap, exposing more ice-free land.

"The children loved the warmer weather as it meant the local river was ice free for a longer period of time, and they noticed that there was an appreciable increase in the fish population. So fishing became a more stimulating pastime and provided extra food for the table. Unfortunately though, they became aware that the changing climate had an adverse impact on the local wildlife. In particular, there was a huge and savage bearlike creature that found, as a result of the warming climate, that it had to search over a much wider area for its food. It gradually wandered down from the South Pole until it infringed on the area where Hepmarkas and his family resided.

"One day the children were out fishing when suddenly their mother heard a terrified scream. She rushed out and was horrified to see one of the huge bearlike creatures standing, watching the children. She managed, with a tremendous effort to control her emotions, and asked the children to drop everything and slowly make their way back to the house. The children dropped their fishing gear and left the fish on the bank of the river. She watched breathlessly as they gradually approached their home. Suddenly the bear decided to attack and rushed toward the children. The mother screamed at them to run, and the children rushed toward the house.

"It quickly became apparent that the creature would reach the children before they gained entry to their home, so the mother did not hesitate and grabbed a broom. She ran as fast as she could toward the bear, screaming at the top of her voice. It hesitated and then moved toward the mother who used the long handled broom to beat the animal about its body. The mother made little impact on the animal, and it threw her to the ground with one almighty swipe of its paw.

"The mother braced herself for the next attack, and just when she thought her end was near, sensed her husband's presence. There suddenly was a powerful surge of energy from Hepmarkas's photonic blaster, and the bear's head disappeared. The creature dropped to the ground, and a relieved mother picked herself up; fortunately apart from a nasty bruise, she was unharmed. The children could only look on in astonishment; they were shaken up but unharmed and totally awed by their mother's bravery.

"In absolute relief, their mother hugged the children until they thought their ribs would break. This was followed by a huge hug from her husband. However, the family realized that the incursion of the bears would be at an increasing rate, and they would have to relocate to guarantee their continuing safety. So reluctantly, the family moved back to civilization although this was at a picturesque town in the middle of the countryside.

"It must be appreciated, Euthymios, that once technological, sociological, and economic advances really took off, there were dramatic changes on my world. This was not of an equitable nature across our planet, and as a consequence, there were a high number of countries that were far less advanced than some of the others. Unfortunately, the more developed countries took advantage of this and grew increasingly richer at the expense of their less advanced neighbors. Hence, there was an unfair distribution of wealth across the globe for quite some time.

"We also had a diversity of religions as well as atheistic beliefs across the various countries, and this compounded the suspicion, resulting from the international competition for world resources and cheap goods. Hence, war between the various countries occurred with increasing frequency and ferocity, and there was much suffering. A very uneasy peace ensued when nuclear weapons were developed. Although on several occasions, we came to the brink of global atomic war, but fortunately through prolonged and usually terse negotiations, conflict was averted.

"In the more advanced countries, spending was prolific, by both individuals and the government; the latter in building up their armed forces and weapons of mass destruction. This reckless spending ran away unchecked, and huge deficits were incurred in each of these country's budgets.

"Meanwhile, the less advanced countries slowly but surely caught up with their more technically orientated neighbors. They found themselves in a superior economic position as they were not spending on weapons of mass destruction and were modest in their expenditure on their armed forces. They also were producing the bulk of consumer goods across the planet due to the exploitation of their cheaper setup costs, taxes, and labor costs. The consequence of this was a spiraling inflation in the more advanced countries as well as high unemployment and a rise in social disorder.

"My relatives, who resided in one of the more advanced countries, watched with alarm as global warming and the ramifications of the huge increases in inflation took effect. The unemployment situation was particularly vicious, and four of my family members lost their jobs. My uncle Agapanthius did, however, beat the unemployment cycle. He was working in a plastics factory, and the general manager of the company announced that due to a lack of orders, the factory would shortly have to close its doors. However, one of my other relatives, Hermondios, was a business consultant and, because of the economic situation, was finding it hard to gain regularly consultancy work. So at Agapanthius's urging, the general manager contacted Hermondios and inquired as to whether he would join the company as a temporary business manager for a twelve-month period. He would have a free hand to do whatever was required to bring the company back to profitability, and in that role, he would report directly to the general manager. Hermondios agreed to the terms and conditions and signed a twelve-month contract. Unfortunately, the brother of the general manager, who was the regular business manager, considered he had been slighted by Hermondios appointment. So he set out to sabotage the improvement efforts that were going to be made.

"The first step Hermondios made in his improvement efforts was to form a company innovation and development team, which included the principal representatives of the company management (including the general manager) and its employees. Together they developed a strategic improvement plan which catered for the active participation of all company employees. This concept covered a rolling five-year period, incorporating a detailed one=year business plan. His concept incorporated egalitarian concepts with an emphasis on the implementation of participative management concepts through the application of self-managed teams. It also catered for the utilization of temporary multi-disciplined teams for the resolution of the more complex issues confronting the company. A participative system of key performance indicators was also developed to measure achieved progress in the key areas and provide feedback to all employees in an open and informative manner.

"The application of self-managed teams proved to be a sound concept, which facilitated the active participation of all employees. It led to improved company motivation and innovation and also productivity improvement and improved quality of output. This resulted in a substantial increase in company profitability and placed it into a strong trading position. However at every point, the general manager's brother attempted to sabotage Hermondios's efforts. He secretly approached the head of the employees union and poured poison into his ears about a massive reduction in the labor force and the forced manipulation of all employees. Fortunately, Hermondios, as part of his employee involvement efforts, had given the union head and the key union representatives a frank and open presentation and guaranteed that they would be fully briefed at key points of the improvement process.

"However, this still did not deter the general manager's brother, and he secretly bribed two of the toughest casual employees to stir up trouble. They were both in one of the key self-managed teams in the company and were responsible for wholesale disruption, which if allowed to go on would surely have had a major negative impact on the whole of the company's participative management concepts. When Hermondios challenged the men, they were arrogant and verbally attacked him. Hermondios stood his ground and calmly responded to their abuse and threatened them with instant dismissal if they did not cease their negative behavior and become positive members of their team. The two men became even more aggressive and threatened Hermondios with physical violence. They circled Hermondios and adopted a threatening posture and moved in to attack him. Unfortunately for the two men, Hermondios was an expert at martial arts and quickly nullified their attack. He then terminated the two individuals' employment and was actually congratulated by the rest of the team for ridding them of two nasty and uncooperative team members.

"Subsequent to this incident, the general manager at last woke up to what was happening and took immediate steps to dispense with his brother's services. Free of any encumbrance, Hermondios forged ahead, leading the improvement activities of the innovation and development team. They undertook a critical examination of all aspects of the company's operations involving the process reengineering of all major business operations. The redesign of some of the key machine tools and the application of group technology were also key strategies of the improvement program. A significant initiative was the introduction of additive manufacturing, which the company was to increasingly utilize as company profitability grew.

"The company also ensured that environmental management was an important company initiative, and every effort was made to facilitate a reduction in global warming when manufacturing activities were undertaken.

"The success of the participative management concept and the resultant record profits continued during Hermondios's first year of tenure as business manager. He was offered the position on a full-time basis, which he accepted, and the company went from strength to strength. In fact, the redesign of some of the key machine tools was so successful that the company opened a new manufacturing facility to produce them. These machines eventually made a major contribution to the company's export earnings.

"A major benefit was that the four jobless members of my family all gained employment with the company in which Hermondios was operating as business manager. In fact two of them became major players in the operation of the participative management concept.

"However, due to the severe downturn in the economy, social unrest was a major feature of the culture in our country at that time. There were massive cuts in the budgets for all civil authorities. The numbers of our local militia, which played such a vital role in maintaining law and order and minimizing antisocial behavior, was cut to the bone; and crime became endemic. Drug taking and alcoholism spiraled out of control; our locally brewed spirits was cheap, potent, and readily available. It was distilled from the juice of a plant we used to obtain a sweetener for a range of beverages and food stuff. The drug of choice was extracted from the juice of the stem of a beautiful plant with large purple leaves and golden flowers. It was considered a weed and could be found growing wild right across our planet. The respective drug dealers and a large number of families grew it as a cultivated crop. When drug taking became increasingly widespread, the authorities considered making it illegal. Undoubtedly the drink and drugs frequently fuelled a multitude of crimes. Increasingly, these crimes resulted in violence against the victims.

"One week, our family had a big reunion, and the members came from across the country and some from overseas. My mother loved these events as, when inviting the respective family members to the reunion, it provided her with the opportunity to conduct long video calls. Hence, she was able to catch up with all of their news, especially those members she rarely had the opportunity to see. When she had completed her calls, you could see her eyes shining, and there was a definite lightness in her step. We had a huge party one day, which lasted until darkness fell. Some of our family decided to go for a walk, to clear their heads and set off at a slow pace along by the blocks of houses.

"Suddenly, they heard a loud cry for help and rushed round the corner of one of the houses to find three men holding photonic blasters. They were pointing them at a man and what appeared to be his teenage children, one of whom, a young boy, was in obvious agony and crying out with pain as he held the stump of his arm. The rest of the arm had obviously been blasted off by one of the criminals' photonic blaster. One of the villains pointed his blaster at my uncle and shot him dead. He snarled, 'You now see what will happen if you do not do as instructed; so take out your valuables and my friends will collect them.'

"Unfortunately for the robbers, one of my relatives was a soldier on leave and, being in the center of the group, was able to draw his weapon unseen. He fired at and killed the robber who shot my uncle through a gap between my other relatives. The other two criminals looked up and in that moment were caught by surprise and that was the opportunity for my relatives to move into action. They used their martial arts skills to kick the blasters out of the two criminals' hands and then followed up to lay them both out unconscious. In fact, one of my relatives, who was not involved in the fray, had to restrain the family members attacking the robbers, or they would not have survived the retaliation by my incensed relatives. Once they had been restrained, my relatives called the local militia on their communication cell devices and watched over the unconscious robbers until the militia vehicle arrived and took them away. The militia ensured that a vehicle was provided to transport the body of our dead relative, and one of my uncles accompanied it to the government morgue.

"The person who was assisted by my kinfolk, although deeply distressed by the injury to his son, thanked my relatives for coming to his rescue. He offered them a reward, which my relatives refused, and accompanied his son to the hospital in the vehicle they had sent.

"My relatives were deeply distressed by the death of their relative. He was a kind and sincere individual and very much loved and respected by all of our family. So they made their way home in a deep depression. My mother took my relative's death particularly hard and broke down deeply distressed and had to be medicated and helped to her bed. They were both very close, and she enjoyed the special rapport she had with him.

"The death of our relative cast a deep depression over the whole of the family reunion. It destroyed all the joy and high spirits generated by our get-together. The funeral was also a sad affair although it was extremely well attended because of our relative's popularity. He had many friends in the community.

"There was another of my uncles, who was very close to the relative killed by the robbers. In fact they were going into business together. This was to market a range of industrial/household water collection and purification systems. The system produced pure water from that collected from local lakes, ponds, quarries, and other suspect sources and was a potential boon in a time of severe drought in so many areas. The collected water was fed into the purification system and distilled down to form pure water for drinking and other applications.

"Unfortunately the purification systems were imported from a country still trying to catch up with the more advanced nations, and the quality of a lot of their products was suspect. The advantage of the partnership of my two relatives was that they were a great match. The uncle who was still alive,

Myron, was a marketing guru and could market and sell anything. However, the relative who was killed was the technical expert, and Myron totally relied on his expertise. So unfortunately when Myron made an agreement with the overseas vender, he did so without any real knowledge of the product and the required quality standard. Hence when severe problems occurred with the product, Myron was totally out of his depth. This was compounded by the severe global recession, which had hit our country particularly hard. Hence not only did he lose money through the problems with the product but also through people's inability to pay their bills. He eventually lost everything he and his family had, and they found themselves out on the streets.

"When on the streets, Myron and his family found just how tough things were. There was row upon row of empty houses, and there was not a house which had not been regularly vandalized by people desperate for money, for food for their family, and also for drink and drugs. It was like a derelict ghost town and to a family as desperate as Myron's family, totally depressing. However, they discovered a house that had not been too badly damaged and moved in until they were either ejected by the authorities or forced to move out by much more aggressive squatters. There was a constant danger that they would be robbed of the meager possessions that they had managed to save and even lose their lives. Fortunately, as a precaution against incursions into their house by callous robbers, Myron had found a secure hiding place in the basement of their new home. On four occasions, robbers broke into the house looking for booty; and as they were on constant alert, the family was able to hide in the basement. However, on a couple of occasions, the robbers were very quick and they were almost caught. One of a group of four robbers, who had really sharp hearing, heard the noise of the family scrambling to hide. The whole family held their breath as the criminals conducted a rigorous search for them and came close to their hiding place. Fortunately, they were not detected, and the robbers eventually left the house.

"It was a precarious existence, and one that the family hoped would not last too long. Myron was urged by his wife to contact his family for assistance, but he knew that they were struggling to make ends meet, and beside which, he was ashamed to admit that he had failed so badly in his business dealings.

"However, the job market was almost devoid of opportunities, and Myron grew weary from trailing the streets searching for employment. His ragged and decrepit appearance also went against him, and he plunged into a deep depression. They were thankful that they could go to the local community hall in the mid-morning and receive a basic meal principally consisting of a lump of bread and a watery soup with vegetables and pieces of meat or fish added. Occasionally, they would also receive a piece of fruit. They were given blankets to keep them warm as they slept. It was not an easy existence as they were subject to a means test as there were so many people taking advantage of the free food.

"One day, while they were standing in a line up waiting to enter the community hall for their daily meal, the man who they had rescued from the robbers came by and saw them. While he was shocked at the family's appearance, he was at the same time delighted to see Myron. He introduced himself to Myron, whom he recognized from when he was rescued from the robbers. However, Myron did not acknowledge the man because he was so ashamed of his poverty-stricken situation. Eventually, Myron broke down and explained his and his family's predicament and how it came about. The man listened patiently to Myron and then explained that he was very wealthy and came periodically to the community hall to give money to the charity coordinators to enable them to continue to provide the services to the destitute. He said that the aid they received from the government was just not enough to cater for the needy, like Myron and his family, who came to the community hall for assistance. The future provision of this aid was also uncertain, as all levels of government were accumulating ongoing debts on a massive scale and were racing head long on a downward spiral to financial ruin.

"The man, whose name was Nicardium, took Myron and his family back to his home, which was a magnificent building, out in the country. When they were settled in and had met the respective staff, the family members were each allocated a room. They then enjoyed a magnificent meal and were allowed to select appropriate clothes from the wardrobes in the house.

"Myron and his wife then agreed that they should contact their respective families and provide honest feedback on what had happened to them and how they were now under the protection of Nicardium. When their families were contacted, they were appalled about their relatives' misfortune, and after initial anger about not being informed, they became sympathetic. It was stressed that if things did not work out with Nicardium that they should inform their relatives and immediate assistance would be provided to Myron and his family.

"Once the family had settled down, Myron was offered a position in the marketing department of one of Nicardium's companies and his wife offered an administration role in the same organization. Their children were enrolled in one of the local schools and soon caught up with the schooling they had missed when the family was struggling to survive.

"Myron made rapid progress in Nicardium's organization and became a senior marketing executive. His wife enjoyed her administrative role in the company, and the fact that apart from the extra money, she had the time to attend to her family's needs. They bought a beautiful home in the same area as where Nicardium and his family resided, and the two families became very close.

CHAPTER 9

Global Conflict and Escape to the Mountains

"Nilandra, Myron's oldest son, discovered that he had a gift for working with computers. He really shone at this when at school and joined the computer club, which provided additional tutorage after classes in the school library. It also enabled like-minded students to bond and form long-term friendships.

"Lymandas, one of the female students, became close to Nilandra. She had a rebellious nature and tended to push the boundaries and try things that were not sanctioned by the school. She persuaded Nilandra to be more adventurous in their after-hours computer activities, and this eventually led to their hacking into the database of miscellaneous organizations. One day, they inadvertently hacked into the site of a known terrorist group.

"To their horror, they discovered that the group was about to release details of the design of a neutron bomb. This was a radically new design of bomb, and it was in the process of development by one of the leading nations. The two students were astounded at the terrorists' ability to hack into the database of such a powerful government and discussed what action they should take.

"It was decided to secretly contact the civil authorities rather than inform the school who would probably punish them for their illegal hacking activities. Hence, they informed the civil authorities, but unfortunately, one of the people informed had a covert connection with the terrorists. The two students innocently provided their names and details of the school in which they were studying to give credibility to their information, relying on the promised confidentiality of the authorities to guard their secret computer activities. So the treacherous agent made sure that he was on the team that investigated the source of the information about the neutron bomb, and that Nilandra and Lymandas's details were provided to the terrorists.

"However, before they followed up on the treacherous agent's information, the terrorists released details of the neutron bomb design to every nation. The terrorists were a radical religious group that believed that the only way to achieve a better world was by global conflagration resulting in the destruction of civilization. The opportunity would then be provided for the few survivors to build the type of world envisaged by the terrorists. There was so much distrust, conflict, and hatred between the planet's many nations, mainly through religious and economic differences, that the outbreak of war was inevitable. It was anticipated that this would result in worldwide conflagration as the major nations took sides in any conflict situation. The terrorists saw their role as facilitating this situation

"To silence the two students, two of the assassins trained by the terrorists were assigned the task of killing Nilandra and Lymandas. The assassins traveled to the school and, before making their move, kept careful watch on the two students to familiarize themselves with their behavior. They also obtained details of Nilandra and Lymandas's after-hours activities by skillful questioning of the other students.

"They decided that the best time to strike was when the two students stayed back at school to indulge in their after-hours computer activities. Hence when everything was quiet, the assassins broke into the school and stealthily made their way along the school corridors searching for the computer room. Unfortunately they were confronted by the school janitor, who questioned what they were doing on the school premises. When it was apparent that the janitor would not be prepared to accept any explanation they would provide, the assassins drew their photonic blasters. Under threat of being killed by the assassins, the terrified janitor told them where the computer room was located. To make sure he did not betray their presence, one of the assassins blasted the janitor, and they dragged his dead body into one of the classrooms.

"The two assassins reached the computer room and entered, looking for Nilandra and Lymandas. They saw Nilandra hunched over his computer but Lymandas was nowhere in sight. Nilandra suddenly found the barrel of one of the assassins' blasters in the back of his neck. The assassin demanded to know where Lymandas was, and although knowing she was in the toilet, he said she was not in school. The assassins did not believe Nilandra and waited until Lymandas came back into the computer room.

"Lymandas returned to the computer room shortly after that time and, luckily through the glass port of the door window, saw the two assassins threatening Nilandra. She ducked down and fortunately was not seen by either assassin. She knew she had to take immediate action but had left her handheld video phone in the computer room.

"She knew she had to contact the civil authorities and also take action herself, as it would be some time before they reached the school and found the computer room. So she resolutely made her way to the staff room and, using a communications device there, contacted the authorities and then made her way to the athletics room. She fortunately knew the combination to the archery cupboard and took out the special bow and quiver of arrows, which she had used to win so many competitions during her time at school.

"She knew a secret back entrance to the computer room and quietly opened it. Fortunately, the two assassins were not aware of this entrance as it was hidden by a storage cupboard. The two assassins also had their backs to the doorway, and hence Lymandas was able to quietly take up position behind them and strategically place two arrows on the storage shelf, ready for insertion in her bow. She selected the first arrow, positioned it in the bow, and aimed at the back of the assassin who had his blaster drawn. Her aim was true, and the arrow went straight through his back, into his heart. He gave a low groan and fell dead onto Nilandra's desk.

"The other assassin whirled round, and in one fluid movement drew his blaster. Lymandas fired her next arrow, a fraction ahead of his leveling and aiming his weapon, and it went straight into his heart. The impact of the arrow caused the assassin's aim to go off target as he fired his blaster just before he fell. Hence, the blast shot past a startled Lymandas's ear and made a smoking hole in the storage cupboard. The assassin then fell back dead onto Nilandra, who struggled to push him onto the ground. They confirmed that both assassins had been killed just as the civil authorities arrived. Their parents had been informed, and they arrived shortly afterwards, relieved that their offspring were unhurt. Both of the parents were too grateful to see their offspring alive and well to chastise them. However from that point on, their computer activities were strictly governed and subject to official school approval.

"Lymandas and Nilandra were upset about the death of the janitor as he was such a friendly and kind individual. He also tended to overlook the long hours the two students spent in the computer room after the classes were over. However, the civil authority's major concern was about the effect of the release of the plans for the new design of neutron bomb. They did not have to wait long to realize that their worst fears had come to pass. Just about every nation raced to build up an arsenal of neutron bombs and to strengthen their supply of missiles and aircraft to deliver them.

"Their internal investigation revealed the treacherous agent's role in both the forwarding of the plans for the neutron bomb and the release of the two students' details, to the terrorists. Through intensive interrogation, the authorities also obtained sufficient information from the rogue agent to destroy the terrorist cell and hence remove any further threat to Nilandra and Lymandas.

"The first incident involving the use of the neutron bombs was over a long-standing border dispute between two of the smaller, less industrialized nations. When the resistance of one of these countries' military collapsed due to an aggressive incursion into their territory by their neighbor, they rushed to purchase more aircraft and missiles. They then moved into action and indiscriminately bombed the opposing armies. In turn, the other nation responded, and soon the incident had escalated into a full-scale nuclear conflict.

"The reason why the neutron bomb was so popular is because basically it is a thermo-nuclear device with a lower explosive yield than other nuclear weapons. This is because the neutrons are absorbed by the surrounding air. It works by using an intense high energy pulse of high energy neutrons as the principal killing medium. Upon detonation, the neutron bomb produces a large blast wave as well as a powerful pulse of both thermal and ionizing radiation. It is designed to kill the intended people targeted while minimizing the destruction of the surrounding buildings and other infrastructure.

"This new design of neutron bomb had refined this concept so that not only was it a more effective killing medium, but it further minimized the damage to the surrounding infrastructure. Hence its release was welcomed by all nations whether intended as a defensive measure or for aggressive purposes.

"It was not long before, through their treaties with the respective warring countries, the more powerful nations were dragged into the conflict. The situation then deteriorated into full-scale global war with very few nations exempt from the conflict. Our country was one of the few exempt nations, but every day we anticipated that our turn would come; and because of this, there was a general aura of depression around our nation.

"Then the war was finally brought home to us when a large country town, in the adjoining country to ours, was subjected to an intensive neutron bomb attack. This was after that country was dragged into the global conflict. The fact that the town was relatively close to their border, one we shared with them not too far to from where we resided, was a cause for real concern. It was especially onerous when we were made fully aware of the full effects of the neutron bomb attack when it was shown in explicit detail on our communications and video unit. It was truly horrific, as we watched the neutron bombs rain down on the town.

"There were massive blast/fire ball attacks all over the town, and men, women, and children were blasted and badly scorched without discrimination and died or were critically maimed. Those people maimed were rolling about on the ground or running round in absolute agony and screaming with the pain of their injuries. The people who were not yet affected were also running around in panic, and they screamed in fear. Unfortunately, a lot of the uninjured people, particularly the maimed, would be dead, either soon or in the longer term. This would be due to the massive wave of gamma radiation resulting in death by agonizing radiation poisoning.

"We noticed how the attack was carefully orchestrated, consisting of strategic, saturated bombing across the whole town. Unfortunately, the efforts of the armed forces and civil authorities seemed noticeably ineffective, and many of the defensive aircraft were either shot down or destroyed before they left the ground.

"It was amazing how very few of the buildings and associated infrastructure was undamaged. When the attack was over, it looked as though people could have just walked in and repopulated the town. However, the thing that stood out, when the neutron bomb attack was finally over, was the enormous number of corpses littering the streets. It was also painful to witness the agonizing cries of the severely maimed who, like the rest of the population who were relatively unscathed, were wandering aimlessly round the town.

"When the coverage of the neutron attack was finished, my grandparents decided to take action. They coordinated a family meeting which was attended by my father and mother, my sister and I, and my father's brother and his wife and his three sons, as well as my grandparents. It was decided that it would only be a matter of time before our country was involved in the global conflict, and we had to leave the town as soon as practicable. We owned two cabins in the mountains, which all members of the family used for their summer vacations. The cabins were well hidden, surrounded by thick forest with open glades that were capable of being cultivated in order to grow a range of edible plants, vegetables, and fruit trees. The forest also contained a diversity of trees and bushes with fruit that was edible or capable of being turned into edible fruit spreads or desserts. There were also bushes and plants whose roots could be used as vegetables in soups or casseroles and as accompaniments to various meat and fish dishes.

"There was a free-flowing river that was fed by a pure mountain stream, which contained a diversity of edible fish and shellfish. They would have to be on their guard when wandering through the forest, as it contained fierce, carnivorous dinosaur predators as well as savage mammal life. However, there were small dinosaurs and lizards as well as wild mammal life that could be hunted and killed for their meat and for the manufacture of garments and whose skins could be used around the cabins.

"The family produced a detailed plan of evacuation from the town to ensure we were fully prepared for our life at the cabin complex. The plan was implemented straight away, and I was allocated the task of collecting the food from the list prepared by the group from the supermarket, hardware store, and other sources. I was to be aided in this task by my cousin Metronobel; she had a keen interest in cooking and was raising three children.

"We worked hard to secure everything that was on the list, and we were finally finished. When we arrived home, we unloaded all the purchases and assisted the other members of the family in their tasks. However, as usual, my mother suddenly found she needed a couple of extra items from the supermarket.

"When we arrived at the supermarket, it was absolute chaos; people were rushing around everywhere and grabbing things indiscriminately off the shelves and pushing them in their shopping carts. There was a lot of angry conflict with people's growing impatience and selfishness. One woman, obviously angry at being beaten to an item by another shopper, was hitting her with her shopping bag. Fortunately, before it broke out into a full-blown fight, the remaining security guard intervened. The angry customer raced past us, and we noticed among other things, twelve packets of breakfast cereal in her trolley. The attendants at the checkouts appear to have fled, probably terrified by the violence of the supermarket customers. Realizing we had little chance of securing the items we required from the almost-empty shelves, we asked one of the shoppers with a loaded trolley what was the cause of the panic.

"She asked whether we had watched the news on our communications and video unit. We explained that we had been too busy to watch, and it was then explained that our country had been drawn into the conflict, and we could expect to be neutron bombed at any time.

"Upon hearing this, we raced home to find the rest of the family, who had heard the news and were all ready to take off for the cabins. We entered the respective vehicles to which we had been allocated and were ready to set off; suddenly, we heard the loud wailing of a siren and knew an enemy attack was imminent. This spurred us on, and we drove like maniacs to get out of the town before the attack. We took the main highway, but it was soon choked with desperate drivers rushing to escape the bombing. Fortunately, the respective drivers of our family's vehicles had an intimate knowledge of the town and its network of roads and streets. So by taking what to all appearance was a tortuous route, we gradually reached the outskirts of the town. This was despite our drivers having to negotiate past other vehicles operated by panic-stricken drivers. Unfortunately, the periphery of the town was being scouted by armed men in open-topped armored vehicles. We waited until we considered it was clear and made a run for one of the roads out of town.

"Suddenly, an open-topped vehicle containing a group of armed men appeared behind us. They yelled out for us to stop, but our drivers put their feet down and gunned the engines to move the vehicles at full speed. Despite this, the pursuing vehicle was still overtaking us, and they fired a shot from a blaster, which shot over the top of one of my relatives' vehicles. In response, my aunt aimed her photonic blaster through the open window of her vehicle and killed the other vehicle's driver. The pursuing vehicle flipped over and rolled several times before bursting into flames. We did not need to stop, as it was obvious that the people in the other vehicle were all dead.

"Fortunately, my relatives had ensured that the vehicles were topped up with fuel, so we had no need to stop on our way to the cabin complex. This was apart from the occasional comfort breaks and to also enjoy some refreshments when we were well clear of the town. So we headed away from the town at top speed and were not quite clear before the bombing commenced. We were hit by powerful wind blasts which really rocked our vehicles, but fortunately, we were clear enough away that we did not sustain any damage.

"We had a comfortable journey toward the cabin area until we came to a tree lying across the road. It was not possible to go round it, so my relatives dismounted from their vehicles and pulled out the tools to cut the tree into sections that could be moved out of our way.

"While this was being done, a vehicle drove up and stopped some distance behind us. Five rough looking individuals jumped out of the open-topped vehicle, three men and two women. They were heavily armed and pointed their guns at us, and one of them snarled that unless we gave them all our possessions, we would all be killed.

"Powerless to do anything, we systematically unloaded our vehicles. We had unpacked about half when suddenly photonic blasters opened fire on the robbers from the bushes on both sides of the road. Four of the robbers were killed, and the fifth one dived for cover. Unfortunately for him, my aunt had picked up her blaster and shot the bandit dead before he could escape.

"When the robbers were all dead, a man and a woman came out into the open, holding their smoking blasters. They informed us that the robbers had massacred the inhabitants of their small hamlet, including the women and children, while they were out hunting. The man and woman had gone to hunt down and kill the carnivorous dinosaur that had been attacking their flock of small herbivores, which they raised for their milk and meat.

"They arrived back at the hamlet too late to intervene in the massacre. Though fortunately, they sighted the bandits loading their vehicles with the items they were stealing without the robbers being aware of their presence. So they followed them at a safe distance, hoping that they could catch them unawares. They managed to drive close, without being seen, to where the bandits had felled the tree and had crept into position through the bushes.

"Our family knew that but for the intervention of the two strangers, we would have all been killed. So we invited them to join us in the cabin area, and they gladly accepted. We then cleared the tree from the road and reloaded our possessions onto our vehicles. The man, whose name was Almanios, and the woman, whose name was Janaous, drove their vehicle; and two of our relatives drove the robbers' vehicle, which was loaded down with goods they had stolen. This included most of the items of value from the hamlet.

"Almanios and Janaous had an intimate knowledge of the area and were able to take us through a number of back roads, which saved considerable travel time. We only sighted other vehicles a couple of times and took evasive action to avoid them in case they were unfriendly. Hence, we reached the cabin area in appreciably less time than anticipated.

"We unloaded our vehicles and then organized the sleeping arrangements. The vehicles were carefully hidden from sight, in case any unwelcome guests wandered into our camp sight. Then we had a pleasant surprise. Almanios and Janaous knew the area even better than any of our family, and a short distance from the cabin site, they showed us a hidden gulley. They apparently had used it as teenagers to have a short break from their families. They camped in a cave, which was situated on one side of the gulley; and while it was quite large, they had widened it out in places to make alcoves in which they had built shelves. The cave was obviously an ideal hiding place if ever one was required.

"The cave, while it was well hidden was also high enough from the bottom of the gulley so that there was no chance of it being flooded. Hence, we agreed that, as well as a hiding place, we would also use it as a storeroom. So we systematically sorted out the stores we were going to store in the two cabins and those we would take to the cave. It was a demanding exercise to transport the goods to the cave, and we were glad when it was finished. The items we placed in the storeroom included our tinned and well-packaged food and the diversity of vegetable and fruit seeds that we had brought with us.

"Almanios and Janaous asked if they could sleep in the cave, as they considered that living in a cabin with us all would be somewhat claustrophobic. We readily agreed, as not only were we dreading having to cater for two extra people in our cramped quarters, but they would be able to guard our supplies in the cave. However to make sure the cave was secure, we strategically planted bushes in front of the entrance, which in time would totally obscure it from the casual observer.

"In the past, the cabins were only used for occasional visits, and hence the cooking and lighting facilities were rather primitive. Oil lamps were used for light and a wood-fired stove for cooking and heating. Fortunately, one of my relative's had marketed solar panels for a living, and we managed to secure enough to service both cabins. We also had brought along a couple of spare solar panels that were adequate to provide light and power to the cave. The challenge was to ensure that the solar panels were erected so that although maximizing exposure to the sun, they were difficult to locate by casual visitors and the wildlife.

"We also had portable generators to provide backup light and power for the cabins and the cave. We had brought plenty of electrical fittings with us, and these could easily be installed by the versatile Almanios and Janaous, who had become highly skilled at undertaking jobs around their hamlet. This meant that we could be environmentally focused in heating, cooking, and lighting the cabins and the cave.

"We were truly grateful that a key part of our stay in the cabin was that, before we left the town, our family had made sure that we were well stocked with all kinds of food stuffs and seedlings. There was also the seeds and plants from the hamlet. Hence under the expert direction of Almanios and Janaous, we grew a diversity of grain, fruit, and vegetables. So we easily had enough for our needs, and to supplement our diet, we would go hunting and also fruit and edible root gathering in the forest. We had to be very careful when searching for food in the forest, as there was always the threat of attack by fierce carnivorous dinosaurs or dangerous mammals. However, a favorite supplement to our diet was the fish and shellfish taken from the river flowing near the cabin area. Our family members loved the outdoor life and became skilled farmers and fishermen.

"Guided by Almanios and Janaous, we also ensured that we rotated the different types of crop to maximize the return from the soil. In fact, we composted everything we could and ensured this was used to good effect in fertilizing the area in which we grew our grain and vegetables.

"A lot of the womenfolk and the men were excellent cooks and ensured we were well fed and enjoyed a variety of meals with delicious sauces and also the most beautiful bread, pies, and cakes. The cooking and baking, as well as the household chores, were undertaken on a rotating basis. This concept was also used for the gardening, hunting, and food gathering activities in the forest. We had captured and penned a number of small mammals which provided us with milk for drinking and cheese making. We also at times killed them for their meat especially when celebrating some special event. Three of our relatives and Almanios volunteered to look after them. Home tutoring of the young folk was undertaken on a scheduled basis by those people with the relevant skill.

"We did notice that one of the effects of the war was that the herbivore animals started to move up toward the cabin area to seek richer grazing on the higher ground. Unfortunately, the carnivorous animals followed them as the food on the plains started to run out. This meant that there was a lot more activity around the cabin area, so we had to be even more careful when going out collecting food, particularly in the forest.

"One day, Janaous was out collecting fruit and edible roots in the forest when a huge bearlike creature came bursting out of the undergrowth. It was an extremely savage specimen with huge jaws and fearsome teeth. It was also equipped with razor sharp claws. Caught by surprise, Janaous stood transfixed as the beast roared with rage and then suddenly attacked. She screamed in fear and agony as she was horribly mauled by the beast.

"Hearing her screams, Almanios raced to her aid after grabbing a photonic blaster from the cabin. He fired a continuous charge from the blaster at the beast until it released Janaous and finally dropped dead. Janaous was covered in blood, and mercifully, she was unconscious; however, blood pumped continuously out of her body, as she lay prostrate on the ground. We carried her into the cabin and laid her down on a stiff canvas sheet on one of the beds. Unfortunately she died before we could even stem the bleeding.

"We buried Janaous in a plot adjacent to her favorite part of her vegetable patch. It was a somber occasion, and an aura of deep depression settled over our small community for some time after that. We knew the death of Janaous could easily be repeated, so we ensured that the necessary precautions were taken from that point on. When any of us went any distance from the cabin, he/she would always be accompanied by a person with a loaded weapon. The only comfort we could take was that, with the increasing number of wild animals, very few people would venture up as far as our cabin area.

"We lived together for a lot of years, following the war and other events on our telecommunicator when the periodic broadcasts occurred. Fortunately as the time went by, the broadcasts became more structured and less sporadic in nature. The war continued relentlessly, and every day, we feared that we would be dragged into it. However, we were well shielded from the effects of any of the neutron attacks on any of the towns near us, and we were away from the center of the armed force coordination.

"One day, to our great joy, it was announced that the war was over and global peace had been declared. We cheered until we thought our lungs would burst and celebrated until late into the night. I must admit that we generously indulged in my aunt's fermented wild berry juice, which is the most potent wine I have ever tasted.

"A couple of days later, my aunt went out to dig up and gather some fresh vegetables, from the cultivated patch, accompanied by her husband who carried a photonic blaster. There suddenly appeared a group of mid-size carnivorous dinosaurs, who were particularly fierce and hunted in packs. There were six dinosaurs in this pack, and the mean-looking leader roared at my relatives. He burst through the wooden fence round the cabin area accompanied by his five colleagues and made ready to attack. My uncle whispered to my aunt to slowly move toward the cabin and then blasted the leader's head, and it collapsed on the ground writhing before it was finally dead.

"The other dinosaurs hesitated, looked at their dead leader, and then commenced to stalk my uncle. He selected the nearest dinosaur and again blasted its huge head. The other dinosaurs stopped and roared, showing an array of long, razor sharp teeth. Once again, this dinosaur collapsed on the ground and writhed before dying, and this time, the other dinosaurs did not hesitate. They fell upon the dead bodies of their fellow pack members, ripping huge chunks of flesh from their bodies and fighting with each other to secure the juiciest pieces.

"My uncle did not hesitate and raced to join my aunt in the cabin. They watched in horror as the dinosaurs tore at the flesh and fought. Eventually, they all had their fill and roared in appreciation at being able to enjoy such a huge meal. They then retreated back into the forest, but we knew they would eventually be back.

"The dinosaur attack caused a lot of consternation, and we realized that this would not be an isolated incident. Consequently, we conducted a family meeting and discussed whether or not we should leave the cabin area and go back to the city now that the war was over. We were evenly split, with some of our relatives wanting to stay and continue to enjoy the fruits of our labor, despite the increasing danger from the wildlife. They pointed out the peace and tranquility and the fresh, mild climate we enjoyed with our relatively high location and also the breathtaking scenery. There was also the advantage of having fertile soil, which produced an abundance of tasty, organic vegetables, grain, and fruit. The river, fed by crystal clear mountain streams, provides fresh water and easily caught fish. There was also the fresh fruit, berries, and medicinal herbs and other produce from the nearby forest.

"However, there were strong arguments presented as to why we should leave the cabin area. It was pointed out that the constant threat from the wildlife would eventually result in some of our group being killed or badly injured no matter what precautions we took. It had been decided a while ago that there was just not enough of us to build a high enough solid wooden fence to enclose the whole of our complex. The generator capacity was also insufficient to keep the fence electrified; beside which, we did not want to put into place anything that might endanger the young children.

"However some of us, myself included, also wanted to experience life in the township. Despite the splendid job my relatives did in home tutoring, (one of whom was a full-time teacher), I was keen to further my education and see what occupational opportunities existed. Two of my relatives of approximately the same age as I was were also keen to explore life in the town.

"We finally agreed that the only way to satisfy each individual's needs was that those of our relatives that wanted to stay would do so. The rest would leave and take up residence in the town and would be welcomed back either for a visit or on a permanent basis if this was their desire. The group that had voted to leave would have a couple of days to consider their decision, and if still keen to go ahead, would leave the cabin area in a week's time.

"A couple of days subsequent to our family meeting, there was a knock on one of the cabin doors. When it was opened, there was a young woman with a small child; both looked completely exhausted. They were taken in and were fed and proved to be absolutely ravenous. When they had finished their meal, they were put into one of the beds, and they both fell into an exhausted sleep. When they were fully rested, they were then questioned.

"They were from the town and actually were distant relatives of ours. They had secretly heard about our move to the cabin area and decided to join us. They said that while law and order had gradually been restored in the town by the newly elected civil authorities, they had a desire to move out to the country and enjoy an open air life.

"Unfortunately, when on the road to our location, their vehicle broke down and could not be repaired. They took whatever they could carry and set off for our cabins. They found a place to rest for the night on the banks of a river. Unfortunately, while he was collecting water for the family, the man was taken by a huge crocodile. The man's wife and young son watched helplessly on the bank, paralyzed with terror, as the crocodile with a death grip on the father, rolled in the water until he was dead. The man's wife and son could only watch in horror while the animal chewed through his body. Realizing they were in deadly danger, the woman grabbed her son and pushed him up the nearest tall tree, urging him to climb. She managed to clamber into the tree and urged her son on until they reached a safe perch.

"They were just in time, and soon there were four of the huge crocodilelike creatures endeavoring to climb up to them. Fortunately they were too high to be reached, but even as they sat secure on their perch, they trembled with fear and could hardly breathe. Eventually they fell asleep out of pure exhaustion.

"When they awoke, there were none of the huge crocodiles around, but they still waited to make sure they really were gone. They then cautiously made their way down the tree and ran for their lives away from the river. It was a harrowing as well as exhausting journey to the cabin area from that point on. They had to be constantly on their guard in case of attack by the wild animals that infested the area. The animal life had proliferated during and after the war, as they were relatively unaffected by the neutron bomb attacks. A couple of zoos had also been damaged, and the animals, including some of the fiercest dinosaurs, had escaped and spread rapidly throughout the area.

"However after reaching the cabin, the woman and her son quickly settled into the mountain life. The woman threw herself into the work around the cabin in an effort to overcome the intense grief she felt over the loss of her husband. Fortunately, with some of us leaving to go to the town, there was plenty of accommodation for the woman and her son. She said that after the war, the euphoria in the town was palpable and there were celebrations everywhere. However, the reality of the situation had set in, and it was realized what enormous problems confronted the town in the rebuilding process.

CHAPTER 10

VISIT OF THE WATCHERS AND GLOBAL RECOVERY

"The global population had been reduced from more than eight to less than two billion people and our town had suffered a similar proportionate reduction in numbers. Hence because the neutron bombs minimized damage to buildings and infrastructure, everyone could be allocated an appropriate home. The problem was to invigorate the food supply and distribution chain and ensure the supermarkets were operating at full capacity. In fact all facets of the supply chain required re-invigoration; people needed clothes and shoes, apart from other vital requirements and medicinal supplies.

"However, it was amazing how thoroughly the civil authorities rose to the task. They not only ensured the general consumer supply chain was functioning effectively but that buildings such as hospitals and schools were fully operational. There was also an expansion in the civil policing units and the new soldiers were given short but focused training to ensure they could effectively undertake their duties.

"Unfortunately, not all of the towns, and especially the cities, were as well prepared after hostilities ceased. Disease and starvation was rampant, and people wandered without purpose around the streets, severely depressed, with a look of complete hopelessness in their eyes. The authorities were stretched to the limit, trying desperately to establish law and order and bring normality back into peoples' lives. Despite the many problems, however, the situation across the globe was slowly improving; but it was evident that it would be a long haul.

"One day, in one of the few operating observatories left operational on the planet, the astronomer in charge settled down for his daily routine of star watching. He was startled to observe a huge starship approaching our planet, Galenos. In a state of great excitement, he informed his young assistant. The astronomer contacted the government official he reported to and gave a detailed account of what he had observed.

"The global war had ensured that all planetary defenses had been completely destroyed. Hence, the official could only hope that the beings in the starship were friendly. She therefore called an emergency meeting of the new government ministers, appointed following the end of the war. The war had decimated governments across the globe, and temporary government leaders had been appointed in every nation. Communications between the various nations was also very difficult as nearly all of the communications satellites had been destroyed.

"So every nation waited with considerable apprehension to see what the aliens would do. They did not have to wait too long as the first move of the aliens was to set the starship up in orbit around the planet. The starship was huge in area, as large as one of our cities and dark green in color. When viewed from one of our cities, it filled the sky, and we gazed at it in wonder.

"The aliens then relayed a simultaneous telecast to each nation's leaders, some via the local news media. The aliens explained that they were known as the Watchers, and they traveled across and between the various galaxies. The purpose of their journeys was to locate planets like Galenos, which had been devastated by a major catastrophe, such as a global conflict and provide guidance and direct assistance as required. They said they wanted to talk to the world leaders to discuss in detail the form of assistance that would be offered. It was impressed upon our leaders that the input of the Watchers was not negotiable, as it was imperative that every advanced nation adopt a path of peace and cooperation before they eventually set out to explore their part of the galaxy. There were many planets with emerging intelligent life forms, and it was vital that peace and cooperation and not interplanetary conflict be introduced to the developing worlds.

"The Watchers' advanced technology enabled them to locate and identify planets that would benefit from their input. Occasionally, they would visit a planet that was in the early stages of its life cycle. Though they did point out that that as long as the planet visited was on course for positive self-development, they had a policy of non-interference. They also pointed out that unless it was absolutely essential, they were reluctant to give any of the planets they visited any of their advanced technology. The Watchers said that they had found, on previous occasions, that to artificially advance the visiting population's technology had disastrous consequences.

"The Watchers then coordinated a meeting of the respective nations' representative leaders. They explained that they would be able to communicate with each one irrespective of their spoken language. To achieve this, they used what they described as a universal communication device. Prior to the meeting, they sent an agenda for the meeting to each leader written in their own language.

"There were six representatives of the Watchers at the meeting, and they explained that a total complement of twenty of their kind was required to operate the starship. The starship was a living, sensing organism and was capable of original thought and action if required, and hence this enabled a much smaller complement of crew members to operate it. The Watchers were an advanced insect life, and dark blue in color. They were approximately the same size as our people but in appearance resembled giant ants. They pointed out that their role was that of process observers, and they would only become actively involved in the process if there was a deadlock situation or where a potential decision was not in the interests of planetary peace and cooperation. However, they could be called upon at any time by a nominated World Development and Governance Council, or its authorized representatives, should that be required. Under the auspices of the Watchers, a World Development and Governance Council was then agreed at the meeting, which consisted of the existing, nominated leader representative of each nation.

"The next thing covered at the meeting was the appointment of a World Development and Governance Council president. We were fortunate that we had Periphemous among the government representatives. He was a highly intelligent, spiritual leader renowned for his wise and insightful decision making. Hence, he was appointed by popular acclaim. It was then decided to vote on the global use of a common second language to facilitate effective communications across Galenos. The debate was long and, at times, quite heated as each proponent of a common language convincingly argued as to why it should be adopted. However after a close vote, a language was accepted, and it was then agreed to use this as the main written form of communication. This undoubtedly made global communications infinitely better than before the planetary war.

"The establishment of a global action group, drawn from the four hundred and twenty representatives of the World Development and Governance Council and from outside the council, where their specialist skills would be required, was then discussed. It was proposed by the Watchers that there should be no more than thirty representatives on the action group. The role of the global action group would be to address the major issues confronting the World Development and Governance Council. This was with the aim of streamlining and recommending solutions for these issues and providing advice for the resolution of the relevant global problems confronting the council. The group could second people with specialist skills, as was required in the problem resolution process. It was agreed that the global action group was not a decision-making body and would refer any major decisions they proposed or written reports they produced to a meeting of the World Development and Governance Council for review and required modification and for final ratification. The decision would then be carried by majority vote prior to implementation action taking place.

"Hence after a fierce and prolonged debate, the global action group was voted in and the modus operandi for the group discussed and agreed. The modus operandi was essentially drawn up to ensure the group were kept on track and did not exceed the limits of their authority. It was further agreed that the members of the global action group would each serve for a three year period. My relative, Hermondios, although recruited from outside the World Development and Governance Council, was nominated as the leader of the global action group as he had considerable success as a business consultant. He was not only academically qualified but also had done a magnificent job in turning a company round and leading it from massive loss to a record profit situation as business manager. Hermondios had also written a couple of highly successful books and presented papers on participative management practices, business process reengineering, and organizational change and development.

"The other members of the global action group were experienced people, and it was surprising that so many gifted people were left alive after the global conflict. These people had diverse experience and skills, which were complementary to each other, and included members with indepth computer skills. The global action group also included two of the Watchers, who were process observers and facilitators and would provide direct input if required.

"It was decided that the life of the global action group would be for an indefinite period of time. However for group continuity, it would be essential that the group members, who were scheduled to serve a three-year term, were not replaced all at the same time. It was therefore proposed that the existing members would be replaced five members at a time each year despite the fact that some of the original members would serve appreciably longer than the three year period. It was also agreed that for relevant assignments, action teams would be formed which would not only contain members of the global action group but also people coopted for their relevant skills and experience. The action teams would work to a specified time frame and would be disbanded when the project on which they were employed was completed. A team could include one or more of the Watchers, depending on the nature of the project to be undertaken.

"The next item on the agenda was the production of a global strategic development plan. It was agreed that this would be the responsibility of the global action group along with the development of an associated set of key performance indicators. A target completion date for this work was set and agreed by the World Development and Governance Council.

"Despite the group's commitment to the achievement of a successful outcome, progress was painfully slow. The global action group members were strong willed, as well as being highly intelligent, and fiercely defended their ideas. The two Watchers, at times, displayed their frustration in an overt and exasperated manner. Their intervention tended to break fiercely defended positions, but in other instances, it took patience and prolonged efforts to move the process along. However, the global action group finally completed the global strategic development plan, and their draft was presented to the World Development and Governance Council for review, to make any necessary amendments and for final ratification. The meeting was a contentious affair, and the president and the two Watchers in attendance were stretched to the limit to bring some semblance of order into the proceedings. However, eventually the global strategic development plan was adopted and the proposed key performance indicator system accepted as a key part of the operational strategy.

"The global strategic development plan consisted of a number of sections, each of equal importance. It was agreed that the objective of the implementation of the plan was to facilitate a worldwide concept that focused on continued peace and fully negotiated planetary development. It was a concept where all citizens, no matter what their color, language, spiritual or religious beliefs, were respected. Where there was a focus on the development and implementation of global economic policies to ensure that poverty and starvation were eliminated and all citizens could enjoy a healthy and disease-free life. It was also a plan that would enable its citizens to take advantage of global employment and educational opportunities to maximize their career development and required individual and family lifestyle.

"A number of strategic development areas were specified. The aim of each one of these was to ensure that Galenos not only moved toward complete recovery but establish a culture of continuous improvement to facilitate a holistic and fulfilling life for all of its inhabitants. To ensure measurable improvement was accomplished, action plans were set in each strategic development area. These were set along with the responsibility and target times for their completion.

"The strategic development area for financial control focused on the requirements for the establishment and functioning of a flexible global economy. This was one that would ensure the continuing integrity of the financial system by specifying the action to be taken in the event of potential economic downturns. It included the rapid movement of finances, labor, and other resources to reinvigorate any potential financial problem areas.

"The strategic development area for health and safety included not only the respective industries but all areas which would facilitate a safer environment for all citizens. It covered the strategies to be implemented for the control of global warming across the planet to ensure complete recovery of the Galenos environment. The days of heavy pollution would now be a thing of the past, as resources were poured into the establishment of such things as nonpolluting industries and the use of pollution-free resources for the production of the energy to power our vehicles, machines, and industry in general. A strategy of continuous greening of the planet was also to be implemented to facilitate open areas of parkland with beautiful shrubs, trees, and diverse plant life. While close control would have to be implemented to monitor our wildlife because of the many fierce and carnivorous life forms, all life would be protected and allowed to flourish in their natural environment.

"Training and development was an interesting strategic development area. It catered for a radical overview of the existing systems. The emphasis, in all levels of education, would be on self-directed learning, problem solving, outcome thinking, self-discipline, spiritual growth, and behavioral flexibility.

"There were several more strategic development areas, such as industrial development, in which Hermondios would play a major role, and infrastructure planning and development. Fortunately, the required development work was less than would have been the case if neutron bombs had not been the principal weapon of war. It meant that the buildings were left almost intact across the planet. However, it would still be a major challenge, ensuring the various cities and towns became places catering for the required quality of life. There was now a total population of Galenos of less than two billion people, and prior to the global conflict, there were some eight billion. Hence, there would have to be a rationalization of the respective city and town sizes and population movement commensurate with overall requirements.

"Once the global strategic plan had been approved, implementation action forged ahead, and the global action group was heavily involved. A key role of the group, supported by the two Watchers was to ensure the global strategic development plan was effectively adopted by the various nations. Then each nation was required to cascade the development plan down through each level of government. It was a demanding procedure, particularly the action planning and key performance indicator system development at the respective levels.

"A key task was to also establish an effective method of reporting back through the various levels of government. In addition, there was a need to collate the provided information to ensure it could be effectively applied as a cohesive and efficient problem-solving and decision-making aid. The principle of exceptions was to be used to ensure that the focus would be on the relevant information required at each of the decision-making levels. The supporting information would be made available as requested.

"It was encouraging to see the energetic and committed way the global strategic plan was implemented. Everyone involved gave it their best efforts, and it was exciting to see the many improvements that were taking place. A key factor in regard to this was that the Watchers had provided small communications satellites to ensure the prompt dissemination of information, across the planet. Unfortunately, there were still areas of dissention across Galenos; one of these was the island known as Alcadia. It was rich in many mineral resources desperately needed in the planet's rebuilding program. It was generally understood that these minerals would be made available to the rest of Galenos as they were required. However, a group of fanatics from the mining community on the island insisted that the other countries should pay a heavy remuneration for this material.

"So one day, the vehicles in which Recemas, the representative of Alcadia on the World Development and Governance Council, and his bodyguards were traveling in were ambushed. The vehicles were completely destroyed by cunningly laid explosives after the vehicles were stopped by a staged accident.

"Recemas and his bodyguards were all killed, and the fanatical group responsible immediately nominated Kyrenas as the new World Development and Governance Council representative. Kyrenas was renowned for his opposition to the World Development and Governance Council initiative in regard to the sharing of Alcadia's vast mineral resources. The council members protested in vain about the dictatorial way Kyrenas was appointed and were particularly vociferous in protesting the oppressive remuneration demanded for the island's mineral resources.

"The World Development and Governance Council secretly convened an extraordinary meeting conducted without the knowledge of Kyrenas. It was decided to send a group of highly trained soldiers, known as a special combat squad, to wipe out the fanatical group who had assassinated Recemas and his bodyguards. This group of twenty heavily armed soldiers had been carefully selected because of the special skill requirements of the mission. Once the mission had been successfully accomplished, the council intended to replace

Kyrenas and appoint a representative of Alcadia who would work within the guidelines of the strategic plan.

"The special combat squad was a tough group, trained to fight and survive in the most challenging environments. This was just as well as there was no environment more challenging than on Alcadia. The climate was hot and steamy with the fierce heat interspersed with heavy, saturating rain. Apart from the one major town and several hamlets where the surrounding land had been cleared for agricultural, general living, and leisure purposes, the island was covered with dense jungle. The squad had to initially negotiate part of the jungle to reach their chosen launching point to avoid being discovered by the terrorists. They were transported to their starting point, a remote hidden cove on the edge of the jungle, by flat deck transporter ship. This was used to transport relevant machines, equipment, and materials round the various oceans and the sea. The flat deck transporter ships also carried ferry vessels which had long armored bodies with movable power ports underneath to lift them vertically on and off the transporter ship and provide powered flight. They were strongly reinforced and armed with powerful photonic blasting units and missile-firing equipment. The ferry vessels could each transport up to thirty soldiers at a time and their equipment into a battle zone.

"The soldiers mounted a ferry vessel and stacked their equipment. When they embarked from the ferry vessel, which had landed on a clearing close to the beach, they loaded up with their equipment and made their way into the jungle. The jungle consisted of a diversity of all forms of exotic plants. Dense green, purple, deep red, and gold bushes; large ferns; and huge palm plants constituted a formidable barrier for the special combat squad to negotiate. The plants interwove, and at times, it appeared they would be impossible to penetrate. A real challenge was the myriad insect life with hidden clusters of large blue centipedes, whose bite was particularly painful as well as poisonous. There were also the many flying insects that administered painful stings. A number of fierce lizardlike creatures infested the undergrowth in search of prey. These creatures were well camouflaged to blend in with the plant life. The favorite prey of these lizards was a smaller lizard which was a herbivore.

"Despite the harsh conditions, the special combat squad pressed on, hacked their way through the dense growth, and made it to the end of the jungle; they all nursed poisonous bites and insect stings. This was despite the powerful repellant with which each soldier was liberally smothered. However without the repellant, they would have been eaten alive and would never have survived the poisonous bites. They had managed to blast the lizards who had tried to attack them without being bitten. So the first thing they did, after they emerged from the jungle, was to ensure the bites and stings they did receive were all properly treated.

"The launching point for the raid against the terrorists was a hamlet occupied by a local farmer sympathetic to the new order. It was on his hamlet that they were grouped after leaving the jungle. He confirmed that the terrorist group all worked in the mines and were located in the southwest corner of the island. This area had long been a hotbed of discontent, and their economy depended heavily on the wages paid by the mining companies.

"The miners and their families lived underground in the old mine workings. This was to not only protect them from the fierce heat and storms, but they also made admirable living quarters. So the special combat squad knew that it would be a formidable task to hunt the terrorists down. The terrorists would obviously retreat deep into the maze of underground tunnels when attacked.

"The squad decided that it was too arduous to hack their way through the jungle to reach the terrorists. They therefore decided to travel by sea to the township where the terrorists spent a lot of their spare time. So they commandeered four boats, each with five soldiers on board. It took them some four hours to reach the terrorist location which, as planned, was late at night. Unfortunately, the night was clear and the light from our twin moons lit up the sky.

"Members of the squad were spotted by the terrorists, who opened fire on the boats. The leading boat containing five soldiers received a direct hit on the engine, and it blew up with a deafening explosion. There was a huge ball of flame, all of which resulted in the death of the occupants.

"The other boats returned a concentrated fire and killed a number of the terrorists. By this time, three more of the squad had been killed and some of the others wounded. However, a significant number of terrorists had been killed or wounded by the fierce photonic blaster and manually operated missile attack by the soldiers in the boats. This caused the terrorists to retreat into the mine workings. The combat soldiers then immediately headed for the beach.

"When they had beached their boats, the remaining combat soldiers gathered their equipment together and bandaged the wounds of the injured soldiers. The four wounded soldiers were left to guard the boats and the remaining eight squad members set off at a fast pace toward the mine workings.

"There was a large opening at the entrance to the mine workings, and the squad members cautiously made their way into it. Two of the soldiers held explosive-detection equipment and two operated handheld thermal imaging devices. The thermal imagining devices detected numerous figures, a lot of whom were obviously women and children. The squad was, however, powerless to do anything to guarantee their safety from the imminent attack. In this case, "casualties of war" was set to become a very heart-wrenching terminology.

"A large number of highly explosive devices were also detected by the squad members, which had been positioned by the terrorists all along the walls of the mine tunnel. The soldiers set their detonation equipment to explode the devices one at a time as they made their way toward the terrorists. Unfortunately, there was an override mechanism covering the quantum of explosive devices to cater for external intrusion, and they all detonated at the same time. There was a massive explosion, which raced through the tunnel with tremendous force. The effect of the blast was to considerably weaken the tunnel walls all the way down the mine workings. Three of the soldiers were buried under the massive rock falls; of the remaining five, two lay injured on the ground. Fortunately, this latter two had sustained relatively minor injuries and were quickly up on their feet.

"The thermal imaging equipment revealed that the terrorist group had been totally buried under the massive rock falls. They had grossly underestimated the power of the simultaneously exploding devices, obviously anticipating that they would be safe from the explosion. Therefore, despite the loss of their comrades, the special combat squad were delighted at having succeeded in their mission and wiped out the terrorist group.

"Unfortunately, the combat squad realized that that there was no hope of rescuing any of the terrorists' family members, who constituted a large number of innocent women and children. In addition to which, there was also a number of the more moderate mine workers. So the initial exhilaration of having destroyed the terrorists was tempered, not only by the loss of their colleagues but also by the large number of innocent people killed.

"The special combat squad then somberly treated the soldiers injured in the mine explosion and made their way back out of the mine workings. When they turned a bend in the tunnel, they were confronted by a large blockage. They strategically placed two of the explosive devices they had brought with them in the blockage. They then retreated as far away from the blockage as possible and flattened themselves against the tunnel walls.

"They found that the resultant explosion had made a large hole in the blockage; however, it was still with some difficulty that the soldiers were able to at last exit the mine workings. The exercise had been very expensive for the combat squad members: only three emerged unscathed, six were wounded, and there were eleven soldiers killed.

"Due to the destruction of the terrorist cell, further resistance to the implementation of the strategic action plan for that area collapsed. Alcadia subsequently became an active member of the confederation of global nations. Their abundant supply of diverse mineral resources played a key role in the redevelopment of the planet. A significant move, in facilitating this was the appointment of a more moderate representative of Alcadia on the World Development and Governance Council.

CHAPTER 11

Final Resistance and a Journey through Time and Space

"The global strategic plan had to contend with further resistance across the planet; but in each case, this was met with decisive action, applied with firmness, flavored with common sense and sensitivity. This resulted in a positive return from the respective action plans in each key development area, and the planet slowly but surely continued to move in the right direction. In this regard, we were fortunate to have Periphemous as the president of the World Development and Governance Council. He certainly lived up to his reputation as a highly intelligent, spiritual leader; and the council members had cause, on numerous occasions, to be grateful for his wise and insightful decision-making.

"Unfortunately there was another major hurdle that proved extremely difficult to overcome. A fanatical religious sect, known as the Hagne, claimed that God had commissioned them to undermine the efforts of the World Development and Governance Council. They stated that they were determined to destroy the council and see the planet breakup into separate states. Their mission would then be to systematically set up powerful Hagne cells in each state and slowly but surely facilitate the establishment of a global Hagne government.

"A major problem with the development of a strategy to eliminate the threat of the Hagne was that one of their agents was on the inner sanctum of the World Development and Governance Council. Fortunately though, through the intervention of the Watchers, the council learned of the Hagne plans and the name of their agent in the inner sanctum. The council also managed to infiltrate the top advisory level of the Hagne.

"When the agent who had infiltrated the Hagne reported there was to be a top level conference of the Hagne leadership, it was decided that that this was the opportunity to strike. The agent reported that the Hagne were to appoint a top level communications company to set up a sophisticated computer and communications system in the conference room in Hagne headquarters. This system would be set up to facilitate effective communications and information searches and feedback. It would also be able to readily locate any hidden internal and external surveillance and listening devices.

"To take advantage of this opportunity, the council secretly selected a group of the most trusted representatives and conducted an extraordinary meeting. They went to great lengths to ensure the Hagne spy did not find about the secret get-together. It was, however, attended by two of the Watchers, who were invited because of their advanced technological skills. A key part of the discussion was how they could use their agent in the top level of the Hagne to bring that fanatical sect down.

"It was a surprisingly difficult task, but the council finally was able to locate a small computer equipment company that could be allocated the responsibility to set a trap for the Hagne. The company was informed that it was decided to strategically hide undetectable explosive devices in the equipment that was to be installed. The explosive devices, after prolonged negotiations, had been secured from the Watchers. They were at first reluctant to interfere with the internal politics of Galenos but realized that they were obligated to support the World Development and Governance Council.

"Through the planted agent of the World Development and Governance Council, the selected computer equipment company was allocated the job of installing the required system in the Hagne conference room. When they commenced their work, the two technicians were rigorously searched and scanned with sophisticated electronic detection equipment. The explosive devices obtained from the Watchers were, however, totally undetectable and were strategically placed in the newly installed equipment by the two technicians.

"However, the covert operator in the World Development and Governance Council complex, for some reason, became suspicious of the work being undertaken in the Hagne conference room. He passed his suspicions onto the Hagne, who decided to take the required investigatory action. Hence when the technician finished their work and packed up, ready to leave, they suddenly found blasters leveled at their heads. They were ordered to drop all of their equipment and hand over their communication devices. They were also informed that they would not be able to leave the conference room until the newly installed equipment was given a full operational test for detection of any hidden video or listening devices, and it was proved that none could be found.

"The technicians were then locked in a soundproof chamber in a corner of the conference room. They were informed that as soon as they were prepared to reveal any knowledge they had of a sabotage attempt, they should press a buzzer in the corner of the chamber. When the sabotage equipment was deactivated then they would be released.

"Despite the fact that the soundproof chamber was quite cool, the two technicians were soon covered in sweat. Sensing his colleague was ready to break down and reveal the explosive devices, the other technician urged his companion to hold on through gritted teeth.

"Some six hours later, the conference room was full of the Hagne leaders, and as there were no hidden video or listening devices detected, the installed equipment was ready to be fully activated. The two imprisoned technicians found the time had passed at an agonizingly slow rate, and they were just about to capitulate. However, the newly installed equipment was suddenly brought on line. This coincided with the technician, who had earlier been cautioned by his companion, furiously pushing the buzzer in the conference room.

"It was too late, and the conference room erupted in a tremendous explosion. The whole building was torn apart by a massive blast and a huge ball of fire, far greater than even the relevant government officials could ever have anticipated.

"There was a long silence among the government officials for the two brave technicians, who had sacrificed their lives. However, their sacrifice was not in vain, and it ensured that the global integration of Galenos could forge ahead.

"The Hagne spy in the government was arrested. He received a long term of imprisonment and, even when released, would pose no further threat to global peace. The Hagne followers drifted away once the leaders were dead and were not heard of again.

"Realizing that there was a need to educate young people to avoid their joining the ranks of sects like the Hagne, the Watchers organized a week-long youth training program. A specific aim of this program was to also ensure a strong pool of knowledgeable leaders would continue to be available on Galenos. This was the first of its kind and was to be the forerunner of a number of similar programs conducted each month. The program would provide training and development to the youth of the planet, and also give the opportunity for them to meet with other young people from across Galenos. It was anticipated they would share experiences and discuss the culture developed in their region of the planet since the war ended.

"The program was conducted in a brand new, well-equipped training and development center in a beautiful valley surrounded by majestic mountains. The implementation of the program of activities for the first couple of camps was to be facilitated by two of the Watchers. They would be assisted by a team of experienced trainers from our planet. It was intended that after the first two programs, our people would take over responsibility for the program organization and running from the Watchers.

"I was fortunate enough to be selected for the first program along with fifteen of my peers. We were very excited about our involvement and could hardly wait for the date of our visit to the valley where the program was to be conducted. The day of our visit at last arrived, and we were fully briefed.

"The week consisted of a demanding mixture of theory and practical experience; the latter making extensive use of our beautiful surroundings. During the day, we were mainly exposed to new concepts and experiential learning. Once we had finished our evening meal, we went over the day's learning and worked on a comprehensive case study we were asked to complete by the end of the week. The program consisted of a mixture of individual, mainly self-directed learning, team work for the external activities and group working in the respective conference rooms. We were encouraged to take the maximum advantage of the well-equipped library and video room in the center.

"The real surprise was that when the week was concluded, five of our members, including myself, were asked whether we were willing to join the Watchers starship crew. We were informed that the Watchers had been traveling between star systems far longer than scheduled. The result was that despite the extensive application of the dilatation unit to regenerate their brains and body and hence enable them to continue to undertake their duties, they had reached the point where this was no longer effective. This had resulted in the death of five of the twenty-person crew because their bodies had just worn out. The other concern was that the organic starship had also aged and desperately required to be rejuvenated at the Watchers' home planet.

"We were all intrigued by this opportunity, and after a long discussion between ourselves and our parents, four of us agreed. The other student declined because the very poor health of his father meant that he would soon be the person to whom the family depended. Hence, the next person on the Watchers' list was selected, a female; our group then consisted of three females and two males.

"Once we had agreed to become part of the crew, we entered the shuttlecraft in which we were to travel to the Watchers' starship and sat waiting apprehensively to see what would happen. However, the engines fired up; and we were subject to a smooth, almost vertical, take off. While called a shuttlecraft, it was actually quite large and was well equipped for a prolonged stay on a planet's surface. In appearance, it looked like a smaller version of the Watchers' starship and was dark blue in color. We asked how the shuttlecraft was powered and were informed that it was powered to take personnel to and from the starship and around the planet. However, it was not designed to undertake flights between the galaxies or through a wormhole in space like the starship. It quickly became apparent that the starship and shuttlecraft were powered in ways that were beyond our understanding. So we were satisfied when informed that the engines could cause the vessel to travel at a speed conducive to a specific journey. What we were told, however, was that when undertaking a journey between star systems, the starship engines could bend time and space and move the starship at incredible speed from the start to the end of the journey.

"Suddenly we were close to the starship, but it appeared that there was no method of entry; but as we moved closer, an opening suddenly appeared on the side of the vessel which was large enough for relatively easy shuttlecraft access. The shuttle bay we entered was quite large and contained another four shuttlecraft, each of which was attached by cables to an individual work station, which formed part of the starship bulkhead. We were shown our quarters, to drop off our equipment, and then asked to attend a debriefing session; after which, we were given a guided tour of the rest of the mother ship.

"The starship was incredible and had a plethora of rooms. There was a large control room which contained a huge dome-shaped central console. It had a large flat panel attached, at a ninety degree angle, to the console wall. This was covered in different sized knobs and smaller clear screens, covering material with strange numbers on them. The panel was in front of a number of large screens showing what was happening in the other parts of the mother ship. There were also a number of solid chairs, with control pads mounted on them, scattered around the control room. These were for the crew members and were used to control the starship when it was not traveling in hyperspace. We each sat on one of these chairs, and they automatically adjusted to accommodate us and to make sure we were each as ergonomically comfortable as possible.

"The starship contained dining rooms, each fitted with a food generating device. These devices could apparently produce any type of required meal and drink. Anyone using the machine only had to put their hands on the device and concentrate deeply on their requirements. They would then wait and a tray from the machine would open up with the specified meal or drink on it. There were comfortable chairs around tables in each dining room. When anyone sat on a seat, it immediately transformed to ensure the individual was as comfortable as possible. When a meal was finished, the plates and cup were placed in an opening beneath the food-generating device and they were recycled.

"There was a technology room containing the dilatation machine and the associated control unit. I and my four companions from Galenos were systematically subjected to a couple of sessions in the dilatation machine cubicle. It was an exhilarating experience, and it was amazing how our minds were opened. The material we covered in our starship training seemed to be so much more meaningful and easily understood.

"The technology room also contained twenty-two catalyst chambers, which the twenty starship crew entered prior to the starship traveling in hyperspace, for example, from one galaxy to another. The two spare catalyst chambers were there in case they were needed, because of problems with any of the others. Entry to a chamber by a crew member was gained by using the gold disk from around their neck; it was placed in a round depression in the airtight door.

"There were also lounges in which to relax, games and exercise rooms, and libraries containing machines that could produce any reading material required. This was either read on a screen on the library machine or a crystal containing the information required could be fitted into the many slots in each room and a screen would appear and light up on the vessel's bulkhead and the information could be read from this. I was informed that the machines in the library could also send the required information straight into the user's mind. It was usual for the Watchers to communicate telepathically, but because of our primitive minds, they used the common second language of Galenos.

"The sleeping quarters were interesting; they consisted of individual cubicles which contained a bed that transformed to facilitate the maximum comfort for the user. They also had study facilities where the crystals could be used or there could be direct input of information into the mind. There was a large screen on the bulkhead in front of the study unit for information recall and which could also be used to send or receive video calls. The Watchers gave each of us a gold circular object in the center of which was what looked like a huge red crystal. The object was mounted on a golden chain, which we placed round our neck. In fact, it is the same object, Euthymios, as the one which I gave to you not long after I found you on the outskirts of the forest. They explained that this was a communication device to send or receive any video or audio messages to anywhere on the starship or planet on which we were located. It would also check our health and warn us of any impending problems and had many other uses, which would be revealed as we became familiar with its use; something which you have discovered, Euthymios. There were also many other wonderful things we saw on the starship, too numerous for me to recall.

"So following our in-depth training, which covered all aspects of the operation of the starship, we were ready to undertake our journey. However, we first dressed as the Watchers; this was in a short tunic of translucent material, which went from our neck, down to just above our knees, and was silvery in appearance. It was a material so light that we hardly knew that we were wearing any clothes at all. You wear one of these garments, Euthymios, and are aware of how immensely strong it is and how it can protect against a sword thrust and arrow. It can even resist penetration by a spear thrust. You will also notice that it never requires cleaning and is capable of interacting with the red crystal around our necks.

"We gathered, as instructed, outside the technology room; and after the code had been entered and the door opened, we entered the room. It was explained that we would each be going into one of the catalyst chambers; these were each like a large shower cubicle, round in shape with transparent sides. We would be gently put into a deep state of suspended animation and stay in that state until we were awoken by the starship. The ship was traveling to the location of a wormhole in space, which we had to enter in order to complete the next part of our journey. The engines would be fully powered, and as the starship traveled, they would bend time and space to move at full speed toward the wormhole.

"We each entered a catalyst chamber, and it filled with an odorless gas, and we were soon in a deep state of suspended animation. I do not know how long I slept, but all of a sudden, I was wide awake and the door to the catalyst chamber swung open. We each left our respective catalyst chamber and moved to our work station and prepared to receive our orders. We were then suddenly asked to make our way to the control room for further instructions. When we entered the control room, we noted that the rest of the crew was gathered there. We were informed that we were very close to the wormhole, and it was intended to shortly commence to travel through it. We would have to move through the wormhole under normal engine power, as the time and space bending unit would not function in the wormhole.

"The lead Watcher also explained that the starship, which was a living organism and could undertake quite significant self-maintenance and repair, had provided a warning about the journey through the wormhole. It emphasized its age and how its general condition had considerably deteriorated since they had first set out on their journey through the galaxies from their home planet. So the Watchers wanted to know whether we agreed to take the risk of continuing our journey through the wormhole to their home planet or take a chance of finding somewhere we could perhaps have the starship completely overhauled. However, it was pointed out that it was extremely unlikely that we would find a suitable planet in which to have the starship brought up to its full operating performance. It was also pointed out that it would be too risky to attempt to return to Galenos because of the distance traveled from our home planet.

"Hence, we did not hesitate and agreed with the Watchers that the best option was to risk the travel through the wormhole. We were then instructed to move to our respective work stations and prepare for the journey; I was apprehensive, but at the same time, a feeling of excitement raced through my body at the thought of traveling through the wormhole to another star system.

"I powered up my part of the auxiliary engine units, and suddenly the starship roared into life and then moved forward. It was not long before it reached the edge of a huge portal in space, the entrance to the wormhole, and dived straight down into it. The initial part of the journey went well, and satisfactory progress was maintained. Then all of a sudden, a tremendous shudder went through the whole starship, and despite its size, it was thrown around like a small wooden toy in a savage breeze. A fierce wind blasted through the ship, and we were all thrown off our feet. We struggled back into position, but the ship continued to shudder with increasing ferocity, and we thought it would tear itself apart. We all were terrified and felt completely helpless with our lack of experience as starship crew members.

"Then all of a sudden, we were through the wormhole, and the starship stabilized itself. The Watchers raced around the starship, checking instruments and controls and looking for any obvious damage, and they appeared exceptionally anxious. Eventually a crew meeting was called, and we were informed that the starship was badly damaged. This was partially because of the aging starship's generally deteriorated condition prior to it entering the wormhole. It was, however, mainly due to the fact that the wormhole was far more unstable than the Watchers had anticipated. While it was anticipated that the starship would not be able to reach Cyrus, the Watchers' home planet, there was a planetary system within reach. The third planet from the sun in this system, enjoyed an environment very much like Galenos, and it teemed with dinosaur life.

"We were each advised to enter our catalyst chamber, and the starship roared into life. It seemed that in no time at all, I was awakened; and upon leaving the catalyst chamber, I looked out of a porthole to see that we were in orbit round a beautiful blue planet. This was your planet, Euthymios, the Earth.

"However, we did not have much time to admire the view before the starship started to shake itself almost to pieces. A loud warning siren also blasted out continuously and was almost unbearable. Suddenly there was an insistent voice in my ear, shouting, "Abandon ship." A Watcher yelled over the top of it for us to make our way to a shuttlecraft and climb on board. I was nearest the shuttle bay and was the first one to arrive and did not hesitate to race into the shuttlecraft that brought us to the starship.

"I switched on the viewing screen and watched the other crew members crowding into the shuttle bay. A huge wall of flame suddenly raced through the bay even before any of my colleagues could enter any of the shuttlecraft. They stood no chance and were all incinerated where they stood. The shuttlecraft, while badly scorched, still appeared to be functioning.

"It was apparent that I had to leave the starship as soon as possible and switched on the engines and short circuited the various preflight checks and headed straight for the starship bulkhead which I knew contained the exit portals. A large circular portal opened up, and my shuttlecraft raced through it, and it was with a sudden relief that I found myself clear of the starship. I headed straight for the surface of the planet and landed close to our cavern complex. This was adjacent to a startled giant herbivore dinosaur nibbling on the branches of a nearby huge tree. The dinosaur gave me a curious glance and moved on to eat where it would not be disturbed.

CHAPTER 12

Destruction of the Dinosaurs and a New Beginning

"I switched the engine off and received an urgent warning to enter one of the shuttlecraft catalyst chambers as soon as possible. It was not long before I knew the reason for this when I heard a sudden roar and saw that the starship was headed straight for the surface of the planet. I rushed to comply with the warning but, due to a combination of my inexperience and panic, did not set the controls and particularly the required timespan correctly for the catalyst chamber. Hence when I entered the chamber, it automatically locked onto the infinity setting.

"Meanwhile, the starship crashed into the planet, traveling at a horrific speed, at an angle to the surface of the Earth. Due to the complexity, tremendous power, as well as volatility of the engines, the resulting explosion was at least ten thousand times more powerful than the total number of neutron bombs that fell on Galenos during the global conflict. The noise was deafening and destroyed the hearing of any creature within the vicinity of it.

"The starship landed in a shallow bay fed by the sea, and the incredible heat instantly raised the temperature of the sea to boiling point. A huge crater was created by the starship's explosion and massive dust clouds and other debris were thrown into the air, covering the earth and darkening the sky. The massive explosion also caused widespread fires, destroying the natural habit of almost all animals on the planet. There were massive earthquakes resulting in the formation of huge tidal waves and the most violent storms ever experienced on the Earth. It was over six months before sunlight penetrated the ground level; hence due to this and the fires, the plants that the herbivore dinosaurs and other plant-eating creatures depended on had died. There was massive starvation of all of these animals, and with the destruction of their prey, the carnivorous dinosaurs and other meat-eating animals starved to death, on a massive scale. This was also the case for most of those animals that lived in the oceans and the sea.

"However, while the dinosaur life was extinguished, somehow some of the mammalian life, including your ancestors, survived. The mammalian life that represented your ancestors then went on to become the dominant species on the planet Earth. The reason for their survival was probably due to the fact that they lived or sought refuge in underground shelters, deep caverns, or burrows during the course of the starship explosion.

"I discovered what had happened following the crash of the starship onto the Earth when I accessed the computer databanks on the shuttlecraft after leaving the catalyst chamber. Fortunately, the shuttlecraft was far away enough from the site of the starship crash so as to not be too badly damaged. The minor damage sustained by my craft was repaired by its self-maintenance system.

"Through the shuttlecraft computer system, I was also shocked to discover that I had been in the catalyst chamber for some sixty-five million years. I was amazed at how I had survived that long in the chamber, and I can only say it is a tribute to the high standard and reliability of the Watchers' technology. It was also a pleasant surprise to find that somehow the shuttlecraft had been able to lift itself up over the years and stay level with the surrounding ground. It had also taken on the appearance of the surrounding rocks and, to all outward appearances, looked a part of the landscape.

"However, I had a real problem, as I had been awoken because the shuttlecraft was about to disintegrate. It should have self-destructed a long time ago but had kept on going until it reached the very end of its functioning life because I was in one of the catalytic chambers. Hence, I had very little time to rescue whatever equipment I required before the shuttlecraft exploded. Fortunately, the shuttlecraft had landed close to what is now our cavern complex.

"Hence, I quickly collected the shuttlecraft's powered trolley, positioned one of the high resolution batteries in it, and loaded whatever equipment I could maneuver onto it and transported this into our cavern complex. I managed five journeys, collecting a diverse number of items including the dilatation machine. This latter machine and the computer and other technical equipment I placed in what is now our technology room.

"On completion of the fifth journey, as I was about to leave the cavern complex, there was a massive explosion. Fortunately, I was well protected by the walls of the cave, but I still waited until the explosion had completely died down before going outside. I found that the shuttlecraft was totally destroyed, and there was no way I was going to salvage any further equipment.

"I went back into the cavern complex and rested on one of the couches I rescued from the shuttlecraft and slept for a long time. When I awoke, I set about establishing a permanent home in the cavern complex. This included cloaking the cavern complex openings, so they could only be seen by use of the gold disk around my neck.

"In time, I had established a comfortable residence, as you well know, Euthymios. However, I was still concerned about my appearance and what problems this would cause when I traveled to the closest village. There was also the problem of transport, now that the shuttlecraft was destroyed.

"However, this was resolved when one day I was on the hillside above our cavern complex. I was looking around to see if I could see any game that I could kill as I was sick of living on the rations I obtained from the shuttlecraft. How I regretted not having enough time to rescue and set up the food production machine from the starship.

"When I looked around, in the distance, I saw a gang of twelve robbers attacking a caravan of traders and their families. The robbers were vicious and ruthlessly killed all people belonging to the group of traders including men, women, and children. Suddenly, one of the traders slung a couple of saddle bags across a horse, jumped on its back, and rode away. Two of the robbers gave a shout and chased after him, and I jumped down and collected a photonic blaster from the cave. I hid from sight and watched while the escaped trader raced toward the cavern complex.

"The trader realized his escape was blocked and turned to face the robbers. He offered them the saddle bags, which he claimed contained all the gold possessed by the traders, if they would spare his life.

"One of the robbers gave an evil laugh and before I could react he drew his bow and sent an arrow into the trader's body. I raised the blaster and shot the robber off his horse and the other robber turned toward me and fired the arrow in his bow. It hit me on the shoulder, but because of the protection provided by the Watchers' tunic, it bounced off. The impact of the arrow knocked me back, and this gave the robber sufficient time to fit another arrow to his bow. However, before he could fire, I had recovered sufficiently to blast him through the chest.

"I examined the trader, but he was in a bad way and soon died. I knew I had not long to wait before the other robbers came looking for their colleagues, so I hid the bodies of the two robbers and gently carried the trader's body into the cave. I looked into the saddlebags, and as the trader had said, it contained a considerable amount of gold.

"Fortunately the trader's horse had remained next to his body, but the robbers' horses had ran off, probably frightened by the noise of the photonic blaster. So I led the horse into another one of the caves and fastened his bridle to a natural rock formation on the wall. I then went out to face the rest of the robbers.

"I took up a position above the cavern complex, which formed a good vantage point if the robbers tried to rush me. I did not have long to wait; the robbers completed the murder of all of the people traveling with the trader and came looking for their two colleagues. I waited until they were quite close and blasted four of them off their horses. The other six looked up at me in surprise, shocked by my lizardlike features. They shouted out that I was a monster from hell, and while they hesitated and muttered amongst themselves, I killed two more of them.

"The remaining four took off, having no stomach for a fight with someone using a superior weapon. I waited until they had collected their ill-gotten gains from the traders and were out of sight, and I followed them. However, before I left to chase the robbers, I ensured I collected a night-vision visor from the cave. I discretely followed the robbers on the trader's horse, ensuring they did not see me. I knew I had to kill them if I was to protect the location of my cave, and beside which, I was determined they would never again murder any honest traders.

"When they settled down to camp for the night, I waited until it was dark and then crept into my place of ambush. They had camped in a gully where they thought they would be safe and there was only one way in and out. I settled in a knoll at the entrance of the gulley and ensured my night visor was in place; this ensured I could plainly see everything as though it was daylight.

"I shouted as loud as I could, and when they jumped up and went for their bows and arrows, I systematically blasted each one. When they were all dead, I made camp for the night and ate some of the robbers' food.

"The next morning, I collected what I considered worthwhile from the robbers' camp and placed it into one of the traders' wagons they had left at the side of the gulley wall. I also collected the horses; they were still tethered where the robbers had left them, harnessed them as a team to the wagon, and traveled back to the cavern complex, leaving the robbers' bodies to the wild animals.

"When I arrived back at the cavern complex, I fed and watered the horses, unloaded the wagon, and put away the gold left by the escaping trader. I then took the trader's body and placed it into the dilatation machine cubicle. While I knew I could not revive him, I was aware that the dilatation unit was a very versatile machine, and I wanted to acquire an exact match to the humans inhabiting the planet.

"When the dilatation controls provided the feedback that the machine had gained the relevant information, I was ready to enter the cubicle for my transformation. I set the controls and entered the cubicle and allowed the transformation process to go ahead. It took three sessions in the dilatation machine for the complete transformation, and when it was finished, I rested solidly for two days while I recovered from the procedure.

"The poor individual who I placed in the dilatation machine and was killed by the robbers, I buried in the hills near the cavern complex. When I traveled back to where the trader caravan was attacked by the robbers, I found that wild animals had torn their bodies apart, and they were scattered round the area. I collected the remains of the caravan members and buried them in a common grave.

"Sometime later, I traveled to the nearest village and traded the horses and also the traders' wagon and goods superfluous to my requirements. In return, I secured the rig, supplies, new clothing, and seed to supplement what I had salvaged from the shuttlecraft; and I also retained the two finest horses for my own requirements. When I returned home, I set about establishing the cavern complex as a comfortable abode, knowing I would probably be here for a lengthy period of time.

"You know my history, Euthymios, do you have any questions?" inquired the Monitor.

"No, master; but I am sure as I ponder over the remarkable life you have led, the questions will arise. However, I think we must first consider what we should do about the five riders I have detected, who are coming this way?" responded Euthymios.

"Quickly bring the vision aid, Euthymios, and we will see if any of those riders are known to us."

Euthymios collected the vision aid, and the Monitor slipped it over his head. The Monitor broke into a broad smile and pointed. "The lead rider is my friend, Alcander. I have not seen him for such a long time; in fact, not since before I met up with you, Euthymios. He was only a youth then and used to undertake jobs for me around the cavern complex; similar duties to your own. However, he decided he wanted to travel, to see what the world had to offer. I had to erase his memories of this place for secrecy's sake but implanted other pleasant ones, and an instinct that when in trouble, he was to return here if he needed help."

Alcander soon arrived at the cavern complex with the four other riders, and they all dismounted; they were sweating profusely after their hard ride. Alcander glanced from the Monitor to Euthymios, looking very confused, and said, "I know that I have been here before, but I am finding it difficult to recall why and what happened; however, I somehow know you can assist us."

"Do not concern yourself about that, Alcander; we will assist you and your companions in any way we can. However, first, Euthymios will take care of your horses; and we will ensure you all have some refreshments. You look as though you have had a long ride, and you must all be both hungry and thirsty," said the Monitor.

Once Alcander and the other men had rested and had finished their refreshments, he explained why he had sought out the Monitor. Apparently, a rebellion against the emperor had been initiated by one of his generals, Nicolardous. While there was a groundswell of popular support because of the brutality and ruthless exploitation of the population by the emperor's soldiers and officials, the general was impetuously charging to meet the emperor's army. He was totally enraged at the murder of his family and had lost all sense of proportion and was totally obsessed with destroying the emperor no matter what the cost. However, it was obvious that the general's badly outnumbered, poorly trained, and equipped army would be annihilated.

Alcander said that he and his four companions were the principal advisors to the general, and they had advised caution and the production of a relevant campaign plan before taking on the emperor's army. However, the general had contemptuously brushed aside this advice and was preparing for a full-blown attack.

The Monitor responded, "Euthymios, take off your robe and the Watcher's tunic I gave you. Your day has come, and it is time to reveal your true identity."

Euthymios did as instructed, and the five advisors gasped when they saw the tattoo on his chest. The royal eagle, jet black, was resplendent with wings outstretched with a poisonous snake firmly in its talons. The words below the eagle could be clearly read, "Truth and justice for all; victory against adversity."

"Gentlemen, meet Prince Evanistas, currently known as Euthymios for his own safety. He is ready to take his place at the head of the rebel army and gain his throne as the rightful emperor of Atlantis," announced the Monitor. "He is also eager to have his revenge on the false emperor for the terrible things done to his family."

The five advisors could only stand, astounded; but even they could feel a surge of excitement, knowing a new era in the life of Atlantis was about to begin.

Printed in Australia
AUOC010649120413
255745AU00003B/7/P